"Don't ...
gosh," Paisley murmured.

"What's the matter?" John-Trevor asked.

"It's him," she whispered. "The crook in the plaid pants."

"Huh?"

"The man you're after, John-Trevor. He's across the room looking at a painting. Yes, it's definitely the man you described. Plaid pants, buck teeth, and he's blowing his nose. No glasses, though. Do you think he used the money he stole to buy contact lenses?"

"Oh, good lord," John-Trevor said, rolling his eyes. "I can't believe it." Paisley had actually thought he was telling her the truth about his case.

"Let's turn so you can see him. We mustn't be obvious about it, though. Remember, act naturally."

"You're the boss." With that, he lifted her off her feet, swung her around, set her back down, and kissed her thoroughly. Paisley stared at him in shock, then sighed and closed her eyes.

John-Trevor smiled. He hadn't planned to kiss her in the museum, but now that he was, he never wanted to stop. . . .

WHAT ARE *LOVESWEPT* ROMANCES?

They are stories of true romance and touching emotion. We believe those two very important ingredients are constants in our highly sensual and very believable stories in the *LOVESWEPT* line. Our goal is to give you, the reader, stories of consistently high quality that may sometimes make you laugh, sometimes make you cry, but are always fresh and creative and contain many delightful surprises within their pages.

Most romance fans read an enormous number of books. Those they truly love, they keep. Others may be traded with friends and soon forgotten. We hope that each *LOVESWEPT* romance will be a treasure—a "keeper." We will always try to publish

LOVE STORIES YOU'LL NEVER FORGET
BY AUTHORS YOU'LL ALWAYS REMEMBER

The Editors

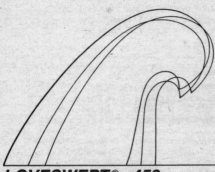

LOVESWEPT® • 453

Joan Elliott Pickart
From This Day Forward

 BANTAM BOOKS
NEW YORK • TORONTO • LONDON • SYDNEY • AUCKLAND

FROM THIS DAY FORWARD
A Bantam Book / February 1991

LOVESWEPT® and the wave device are registered
trademarks of Bantam Books, a division of
Bantam Doubleday Dell Publishing Group, Inc.
Registered in U.S. Patent
and Trademark Office and elsewhere.

If you would be interested in receiving protective vinyl
covers for your Loveswept books, please write to this
address for information:

Loveswept
Bantam Books
P. O. Box 985
Hicksville, NY 11802

ISBN 0-553-44098-5

Published simultaneously in the United States and Canada

Bantam Books are published by Bantam Books, a division
of Bantam Doubleday Dell Publishing Group, Inc. Its trademark, consisting of the words "Bantam Books" and the
portrayal of a rooster, is Registered in U.S. Patent and
Trademark Office and in other countries. Marca Regis-
trada. Bantam Books, 666 Fifth Avenue, New York, New
York 10103.

PRINTED IN THE UNITED STATES OF AMERICA

OPM   0 9 8 7 6 5 4 3 2 1

For Evelyn and Michele Seranne
Thank you, friends

The dictates of the heart
are the voice of fate.
> —JOHANN CHRISTOPH
> FRIEDRICH VON SCHILLER
> 1759–1805

Prologue

John-Trevor Payton took a sip of brandy from the fragile, hand-blown snifter, savoring the sensation of the expensive liquor caressing his throat like warm velvet. He held the snifter at eye level and watched the light from the leaping flames of the fire dance with changing colors through the amber liquid. Taking another sip, he chuckled.

"Colonel," he said, "this brandy makes coming to your godforsaken mountain worth the trip every time."

The white-haired man sitting opposite John-Trevor in a matching butter-soft leather chair raised his glass in salute.

"I like a man who appreciates fine brandy," Col. William Blackstone said, "and you've earned it. Being stranded in Denver for two days because of that blizzard, and now spending New Year's Eve with an old man instead of being at a party, is above and beyond the call of duty."

"I've attended my share of New Year's Eve parties," John-Trevor said. "I'm very comfortable and contented here. But . . ."

"But you're eager to know just why I sent for you this time."

"Yes," John-Trevor said, nodding. "I'm sure it wasn't so that I could deplete your supply of fantastic brandy."

Colonel Blackstone sighed, then stared into the fire for several long minutes before speaking again.

"John-Trevor," he said finally, "I'm an old man. That can't be ignored."

"Seventy-five isn't that old," John-Trevor said.

"Seventy-five," Colonel Blackstone repeated. "Where did all the years go? I sit here in my five-million-dollar house, knowing I'm an extremely wealthy man, and I envision myself as a big, strapping fellow like you. Young, full of life, ready to take on whatever comes next. But I'm old, dammit, and I've got the aches and pains to prove it."

John-Trevor nodded, not knowing what to say.

"But you're not interested in my creaking bones," the colonel went on. "You want to know the reason for my asking you to come here."

John-Trevor rolled his snifter between his hands and waited for the colonel to continue.

"Over twenty-five years ago," Colonel Blackstone said, "I fell in love. It was the first and last time that I ever truly loved a woman. I met her in Paris where she was singing bawdy songs in a nightclub. Her name was Kandi Kane."

"Pardon me?" John-Trevor said.

The colonel laughed softly. "Terrible, isn't it? It was a stage name, of course. Kane was really her last name, but she added the Kandi. Kandi Kane. Lord, she was beautiful. She had black, silky hair that flowed to her waist, and the darkest eyes I've ever seen. Her skin was like alabaster. . . ."

The colonel fell silent, lost in his memories. John-Trevor waited patiently.

"Yes, well," the colonel said, sitting up straighter in his chair. "Kandi wasn't French. She was an American, in fact, but she adored Paris. She was wild and reckless, lived every minute of her life to the fullest, and was as elusive as the wind as far as commitment went. Never, she vowed, would she settle down with one man, stifle her zest for life. I saw her steadily for a year, whenever my busy schedule allowed me to get to Paris. She was always delighted to see me, acted as though she'd been waiting just for me. I finally asked her to marry me, but she refused, and soon after she said that what we'd had together was over."

"And you agreed?"

"Not immediately, no. You have to understand, John-Trevor, I'm a man who's been accustomed to winning. I was a tough negotiator in my day, perfectly willing to walk away from a deal if it wasn't put together the way I wanted it. At the time Kandi said our affair was finished, I'd just completed a multimillion-dollar land purchase in Texas that eventually produced several oil wells." He smiled at the memory. "Outbid a couple of very powerful men who were after that land, and finally started earning some respect. It had been a long time coming for a dirt-poor boy raised on a run-down Colorado ranch."

"And you still like thumbing your nose at all those so-called financial geniuses. I remember the ruckus a few years ago when you bought a thirty-five-floor skyscraper in midtown Manhattan right out from under the noses of the kings of New York real estate."

The colonel nodded. "Yes, that was a sweet victory. I've lost count of how many coups I've pulled off. And twenty-five years ago, it never occurred to me that I couldn't change Kandi's mind about marrying me."

"But?"

"But nothing moved her. I had flowers delivered to her morning, noon, and night, chauffeured her to and from the nightclub. I took her to the finest restaurants. I hired a realtor to start looking for property on the French Riviera. I had the best designer in France make an entire wardrobe for her. I promised her the world."

"And she turned you down?"

"Yes, and with no hesitation. When I foolishly persisted, presenting her not only with a diamond ring, but with a diamond necklace and earrings, too, she finally became angry. She handed them back to me and told me that she couldn't be bought, that simply because I had money and power didn't mean I could have her too. She said I was tarnishing the lovely memories she had of our times together, and that was making her unbearably sad. As unbelievable as it was to me, I realized I had lost. Kandi Kane was not mine to have."

"That's rough," John-Trevor said.

"Very. I left Paris and didn't see her again, but I've never forgotten her. Never. Now, the past, after all these years, has come into my present."

John-Trevor leaned forward, resting his elbows on his knees, his gaze fixed on the colonel.

"About a year ago," the older man said, "when I finally retired, I found myself taking stock of my life more and more often. Always there, in the forefront of my thoughts, was Kandi. I knew I had to find out if she was all right, happy, had what she needed. And also present was the fervent hope that she still had deep feelings for me, that we could, at long last, be married, and I could spend my last years with her. I hired a Parisian detective to locate her."

"Did he find her?"

Colonel Blackstone drew in a shaky breath. "Yes. Kandi was killed in an automobile accident five years ago. It took the detective months to discover that."

"Oh, Lord," John-Trevor said, shaking his head. "I'm sorry."

"The detective dug deeper in order to provide me with a full picture of what Kandi's life had been like since the last time I saw her. He managed to find, and gain the confidence of, people who had known her, cared about her. From them he gathered many missing pieces to the puzzle. I received his report several weeks ago and have sat here in this big, echoing place mourning the loss of Kandi, reliving memories of our wonderful days together. But now it's time to put aside my grief and take action."

"What kind of action?"

"John-Trevor, I have a daughter who is nearly twenty-four years old, a child I created with Kandi."

"She never told you she was expecting your baby?" John-Trevor asked, raising his eyebrows.

"No, but that doesn't surprise me. Kandi would do nothing to threaten her independence. I would have moved heaven and earth to be a part of my child's life, and Kandi knew that. However, according to Kandi's friends, she felt that when our child was of age, she had the right to know who her father was. She planned to tell the young woman my identity on her twenty-first birthday."

"But she was killed before your daughter turned twenty-one."

"Exactly. The detective's report states that for several years Kandi was bitter and angry about how I'd tried to persuade her to marry me, how I'd tried to buy her, as though I wanted to add her to my collection of cars, my land, my businesses. She was also, her friends said, extremely hurt."

The colonel shook his head, frowning, then continued, "As the years passed, Kandi finally chose to remember the special, beautiful times we'd shared, rather than concentrate on my blundering exit from her life. She was constantly sought after by men, and when several others attempted, from her viewpoint, to buy her, she became even more wary of men with money. She refused even to have a drink with a man she deemed as too devoted to the pursuit of money."

"Unusual," John-Trevor said.

"Oh, she was that," Colonel Blackstone said, smiling. "So unique. So beautiful." He paused. "And despite her much-vaunted need for independence, I've been assured that she was a devoted mother. Her friends say that after her daughter was born, she was first in Kandi's life.

"John-Trevor, Kandi intended to tell our daughter who I was. As the child's father, I feel the responsibility of that decision now rests on my conscience. I have convinced myself that Kandi would have told me about our daughter at the same time she revealed my name to her."

John-Trevor nodded. "I'd say that's a fairly safe bet."

"More than ten years ago," the colonel went on, "Kandi purchased a house in Denver. Real estate prices were very low then. She made a small down payment and used all her savings to place enough funds in escrow to make the mortgage payments for the years remaining until our daughter's twenty-first birthday. The house was left to our child in Kandi's will."

"I get the picture," John-Trevor said. "She was trying to move her daughter, *your* daughter, close to you. She would have presented the opportunity for your daughter to live in America if she wanted to as part of her birthday present. The other gift would be the name of her father."

"That's correct. If that child chose not to live in Denver, then it would be a sign that I was never to meet her. Kandi always believed in fate, in things happening as they should without undue outside influence."

"I see. Colonel, I have to ask you this. How can you be certain that you're the father?"

"Because Kandi says I am. She was the most honest woman I've ever known. Oh, yes, John-Trevor, that young lady is my daughter, and she's living in the house in Denver."

"Where do I come in? You've apparently already found out what you need to know. She's down in Denver, she's your daughter. I don't see where there's anything left for me to do."

"But there is. It's up to me to decide whether or not I should tell our daughter of my existence. She might be better off, happier, if she never knows my identity—*and* if she didn't receive the millions of dollars, the real estate, the controlling interest in my businesses, all she would inherit from me."

"That's a difficult decision, Colonel."

"Indeed, it is, and that's why you're here. I want you to get to know my daughter, discover everything you can about her, to help me make the right decision. I have her address. You're to leave for Denver first thing in the morning." He paused, gazing at the fire. "How strange it is to realize that I've been sitting up here on my mountain only forty miles from my only child, not even knowing she existed. I may never meet her." He looked back at John-Trevor, fixing him with a steady gaze. "That will depend on what you report to me. *Her* needs will be my first consideration. Money, John-Trevor, often destroys more lives than it benefits. I will do nothing to cause my daughter unhappiness."

"I understand," John-Trevor said. "I'll be as objective as possible, Colonel. I'll give you facts without opinion."

"Take all the time you need. This is too important to be rushed. Keep in touch, but I won't put a deadline on you."

"Fair enough. I'll leave in the morning. What's your daughter's name, Colonel?"

"Paisley. Paisley Kane."

One

"Look Out! Clear the way! My motor's stuck! Everybody mo-o-o-ve!"

John-Trevor heard a woman scream the frantic warnings as he approached the corner on the icy sidewalk. He peered around the end building and quickly scanned the street, assuming that if a motor was stuck, a vehicle was in trouble.

"Oh-h-h, no-o-o!" the woman yelled.

John-Trevor snapped his head around— and instantly was hit full force by a whizzing something clad in red. A second later he was on his back in a wet, cold snowdrift on the edge of the sidewalk, the creature in red stretched out on top of him.

He blinked, drew some much-needed air into his lungs, and realized it was a woman pinning him down. Still dazed, he stared fixedly at her face . . . a beautiful face, with eyes so dark they were nearly black, skin like white satin, a pert nose, and a tempting mouth that was only inches from his. She was wearing a red down jacket and a red knit cap. Dark curls peeked around the brim of the hat, and long lashes framed her big eyes.

He was in the right neighborhood, John-Trevor mused, and the description definitely fit. He had the sneaky suspicion that this delectable bundle was none other than Miss Paisley Kane.

"Hi there," she said, smiling brightly. "I'm Paisley Kane." A frown replaced the smile. "And I'm very sorry that I knocked you down. Are you all right? I really am sorry, but my motor stuck, you see, and there I was zooming along the sidewalk, and then there you were, and . . . well, here we are."

"Yep," he said, smiling, and not at all surprised that his hands had settled at her waist, holding her lightly. "Here we are. I'm John-Trevor Payton," he added.

"How do you do?" she said politely. "Oh, no, forget that. You were doing fine until my motor got stuck. If you'd, shall we say unhand me, Mr. Payton, we can both get out of this snow."

"It's John-Trevor," he said, "with a hyphen."

"Really? I like your name. It has a rather French sound to it."

"That's what my mother thought. She was French, and my brothers and I all got hyphenated names. Paul-Anthony, James-Steven, and me."

She smiled. "That's delightful. I was born in Paris myself, though I'm not French. I adore Paris, but I like Denver, too, of course. I think that's because it's so totally different from Paris. I've lived here for five years. My, time does fly, doesn't it?"

John-Trevor chuckled, causing Paisley to bounce slightly on his chest.

"You're rather adept at flying yourself, Miss Paisley Kane. It is 'Miss,' isn't it?"

"Oh, yes. I'm not married. Are you?"

"Nope, and I have no intention of ever marrying."

"Ah, one of those," she said, nodding. "A confirmed bachelor. Well, to each his own. You're deliciously handsome, John-Trevor. Are you a playboy?"

"What?" he said with a burst of laughter.

"No, never mind, it's none of my business. Well, it's been nice talking with you, but I really think we should get up and out of this snowdrift. I, for one, am freezing to death."

Paisley Kane was like a breath of fresh air, John-Trevor thought. She seemed to say whatever came to her mind, chattering blithely like a magpie. She was really something, this lovely daughter of Colonel Blackstone.

"Hello?" she said.

"Oh, right," he said, and, as he spoke, realized he didn't want to let her go. She felt so damn good nestled against him, even with the layers of bulky clothing separating them. If he lifted his head, he could capture her kissable lips with his and—

"You bet," he said, and reluctantly released his hold on her.

Paisley shifted off him and got to her feet, then stood motionless for a moment, gazing down at him. How strange, she thought. She had *liked* lying on top of John-Trevor Payton, even in a snowdrift. Insane, that's what it was. He was a total stranger. But still, he was sinfully gorgeous. He had wonderful hair, dark auburn and thick, and his eyes were amazingly blue, like a summer sky. Handsome, he didn't have the elegant, refined attractiveness of men she'd known in Paris. He had the strong, rugged good looks she'd found only in American men. There was a lot of him too. His heavy sheepskin jacket couldn't disguise his wide shoulders and broad chest, and despite their winter clothes, his body had felt hard, muscular when she'd landed on top of him.

John-Trevor rolled to his feet, and Paisley stepped back, embarrassed to have been staring so blatantly. The sound of someone running caught her attention, and she turned to see a man hurrying down the sidewalk toward them. She glanced at John-Trevor and wasn't surprised to see him gaping at the man. About sixty years old and wearing an oversize, shabby black coat and a floppy felt fedora that had seen better days, the professor did cut an odd figure.

"Paisley, Paisley," he said, coming to a breathless halt in front of her and John-Trevor, "what happened?"

"My motor stuck," she said cheerfully. "Professor, this is John-Trevor Payton. John-Trevor, meet Professor Kling."

"Yes, yes, hello," the older man said absently. He leaned over and peered at Paisley's feet. "Mmm."

When Paisley did the same thing, John-Trevor shrugged, planted his hands on his knees, and looked down. Paisley had small boards strapped onto the bottom of her boots.

"Motorized skis," she said to him. "The sidewalks get very icy here, you see, and the professor invented these as a means of getting from here to there." She took a small black box from her jacket pocket and sighed. "I'm afraid they need a tad more work, Professor. My motor stuck."

Professor Kling stroked his chin. "I must investigate this right away." He took the box from her, unbuckled the mini-skis, took them off, and tucked them under one arm. "Just a minor setback," he mumbled. "I'll reevaluate the situation, sweet Paisley."

"Bye, Professor," she said. "I'll see you later."

As the professor scurried away, John-Trevor stared after him.

"Is he for real?" he asked.

Paisley smiled. "He's an inventor. You

wouldn't believe some of the things he's invented." Her smile changed into a frown. "He has a great many problems, though, poor dear. Nothing ever seems to work quite the way he planned."

"No joke," John-Trevor said. "You could have been badly injured on those crazy skis."

"No, I would have landed in that snowdrift, safe and sound. I really admire the professor because he never gives up. He suffers one defeat after another and keeps on keeping on, as the saying goes. I never know what he'll produce in my basement."

"He works in your house?"

"Yes, the basement is his private laboratory. No one is allowed down there. He has one of the bedrooms, of course, but the man hardly sleeps. He's amazing."

"You run a boardinghouse?"

"Well, no, not exactly. That is, I didn't set out to, but it sort of happened because I kept meeting people who had nowhere to go and . . ." She shrugged. "I had plenty of room, so . . . Anyway, I for one would like to get inside and get warm and dry. Since it's my fault that you're no doubt freezing in those wet clothes, would you like to come to the house and stand by the fire for a bit?"

"Absolutely. After you, ma'am," John-Trevor said with a sweep of his arm.

As they walked along the icy sidewalk, John-Trevor noted that the neighborhood comprised a series of small storefronts as well as old two-

and three-story houses. Some of the buildings were well tended to, while others gave evidence of the ravages of time.

"Hi, Paisley," a tall, thin man said as he passed them.

"Hi there, Chunky," she said. "How's the book coming along?"

"I'm communing with my muse," he said over his shoulder.

"Good for you," Paisley called back. She looked up at John-Trevor. "That was Chunky. I met him right after I moved here. He lives over that little market we just went by. He's been communing with his muse for five years that I know of. So far, not one word of his book has been put on paper. Someday, though, he's going to write a brilliant novel. I can feel it in my bones. I've never asked him what his real name is. Oh, let's hurry. I'm so cold."

Yes, Paisley Kane was really something, John-Trevor thought. Rather exhausting, but definitely refreshing. She seemed to accept people just as they were, passing no judgment on them or how they conducted their lives. Had she learned that from her mother? Probably. Kandi Kane would have had to have been a very special woman to win the heart and love of Colonel Blackstone.

"This is my home," Paisley said, turning into a yard.

John-Trevor quickly scanned the house. Two stories high and painted pale blue with white shutters, it was obviously well cared for. A low, white wooden fence edged the yard, and the walkway leading to the wide front porch was free of ice and snow. A flash of color caught his eye, and he glanced at the front door. Narrow panels of clear glass flanked the wooden door, except for a rectangle of stained glass on one side, the different colors in diamond shapes. How unusual, he thought, wondering if the stained glass was Paisley's.

"Nice place," he said. "I bet you have flowers growing in the spring."

"Dozens of them. How did you know?"

He shrugged. "It fits the picture, that's all."

They went up the three steps to the porch, then Paisley stopped at the front door and glanced up at him.

"Flowers fit the picture?" she asked, cocking her head slightly. "Oh, you mean the final touch to the house."

"No, Paisley." He looked directly into her dark eyes, and his voice deepened. "I mean the image of *you*. You and bright spring flowers just seem . . . to go together."

She smiled. "What a lovely thing to say. Thank you, John-Trevor."

Neither moved. Cold, wet clothes were forgotten, as warmth spread through them, as real as the spring sunshine that would nudge the flowers awake from their long sleep of winter.

Paisley's heart began to race, and she felt an unfamiliar pulsing heat low in her body.

What would it be like, she wondered, to be kissed by John-Trevor Payton? Would he haul her into his arms and kiss her fiercely, or would his embrace, his kiss, be tempered with gentleness? Oh, *mon Dieu,* where were these wayward thoughts coming from?

She tore her gaze from his and pulled open the storm door, hoping he didn't notice the deep, shaky breath she took. Before turning the knob on the inner wooden door, she touched the fingertips of one hand to the stained-glass window beside it. Then she opened the door and walked into the house with John-Trevor right behind her.

Lord, he thought, he'd been a breath away from hauling Paisley into his arms and kissing her fiercely. When she'd stood there gazing at him, he'd felt as though he were drowning in the dark depths of her eyes. The urge to hold her, to kiss her and taste her, had been nearly irresistible.

Dammit, what was she doing to him? He was there to do a job, which he'd do well to remember. Paisley Kane was off-limits, part of an assignment and the daughter of a man he highly respected. He was going to get his act together . . . right now.

As Paisley closed the door, he looked at the stained-glass panel, approximately one foot wide and two feet long.

"That's really very striking," he said, unbuttoning his coat. "I saw you touch it before we came in. Do you always?"

"Yes." She shrugged out of her down jacket and hung it on a brass coat tree by the door. "It's an automatic gesture. I wasn't even aware I did it."

"Why do you? Some sort of good luck charm?"

"No, not really. You see, it belonged to my mother. It was her most cherished possession. No matter where we lived, she always found a place to put it where the sun would shine through and create vibrant rainbows in a room. When she died five years ago, the glass became *my* most precious treasure because of her."

He nodded. "So, that's why you touch it. It's your link to your mother."

"Yes, but it's more than that. It's . . . well, you really should get out of that wet coat."

She took off a heavy blue sweater, then the green one she wore beneath it, and tossed them onto the coat tree as John-Trevor hung up his own jacket.

"Why don't you go stand by the fire?" she said, gesturing to the open doorway behind him that led to the living room. "I'll make hot chocolate if you'd like it."

"Okay." John-Trevor hesitated, then drew one thumb over Paisley's cheek. "Thank you for inviting me to share your fireplace and hot chocolate."

She nodded, then stepped back, forcing him to drop his hand. She turned and walked down the hall toward the back of the house.

John-Trevor watched her, realizing that without the bulky clothes, Paisley was small boned and delicate. She was maybe five feet four and had a trim figure with small breasts and a nicely rounded bottom.

She was wearing jeans with a splash of bright, embroidered flowers down the side of each leg, and he wondered if she'd sewn the intriguing addition herself. Matching flowers tumbled across the front of her yellow sweat-shirt, as though blown there by a playful summer breeze.

He looked back at the stained-glass panel for a long moment, then walked into the liv-ing room. Standing with his back to the warm fire, he surveyed the room, searching for other clues to this enchanting woman.

The room was large with braided rugs on gleaming hardwood floors. The furniture was an intriguing blend of what he guessed were Victorian-era antiques and a few modern pieces. It was a comfortable room, welcom-ing, despite its jumble of styles. The room *was* Paisley—saying, doing, whatever came to mind at the moment.

Noticing a small photo album lying beside him on the mantel, he started to reach for it when her voice stopped him.

"Here we go," she said, entering with a tray that contained two mugs and a plate of sugar cookies.

"That didn't take long," he said.

She laughed. As the happy sound filled the room, John-Trevor found himself smiling . . . and found his heartbeat quickening, a sudden desire tightening his body.

"My secret recipe for hot chocolate is very quick to prepare," she said as she set the tray on the coffee table. She turned to study him. "Let's see, should I share my recipe with you? Do I trust you, John-Trevor Payton? Would I buy a used car from this man?" She waved one hand breezily in the air. "Sure. Why not?" She sat down on the sofa and patted the cushion next to her. "Come sit and have some of this delicious brew."

He settled next to her, then leaned over to peer into the mugs.

"I think I'll wait," he said, "until you tell me the recipe before I try it."

"O ye of little faith," she said, wrinkling her nose. She glanced around the room as though looking for recipe thieves. "Okay, here it is. The recipe." She lowered her voice to a confiding whisper. "You buy a quart of chocolate milk, pour it into a pan, and heat it up. Voilà! Hot chocolate."

John-Trevor laughed. He turned his head to meet Paisley's gaze, and a message instantly hammered against his brain. If he didn't kiss Paisley Kane, he was going to lose his ever lovin' mind.

Their smiles faded; their gazes held fast.

"Paisley," John-Trevor said, his voice

sounding strangely raspy to his own ears, "I'm going to kiss you."

"That's a splendid idea."

He framed her face in his hands and covered her mouth with his, parting her lips, seeking and finding her tongue. She wound her arms around his neck and fully answered the demands of his kiss.

Desire exploded within John-Trevor. Heat rocketed through him, causing his manhood to surge. Paisley's taste was sweet nectar, her aroma was fresh air and flowers.

The kiss was sensational—and the kiss shouldn't have been happening because he was investigating her, had to maintain his objectivity. He was going to end this kiss . . . in a week or so.

Ça, c'est incroyable, Paisley thought dreamily. She'd never been kissed like this. Never. She felt strange, as though she were floating up and out of herself to a sensual paradise she hadn't known existed. She was acutely aware of every inch of her own body, as well as John-Trevor's. The kiss was heavenly, and she wanted it to go on and on and—

John-Trevor raised his head, dropping his hands from her face and straightening. She opened her eyes and sighed.

"Oh, John-Trevor," she murmured breathlessly. "That was . . . that was marvelous. When you kiss a person, you really kiss a person. Absolutely marvelous."

"Right," he said gruffly, and picked up one of the mugs.

He took a swallow of the hot chocolate, then cradled the mug in both hands, his elbows resting on his knees. He frowned as he stared into the crackling flames of the fire.

Paisley looked at him for a long moment before reaching for her mug and taking a sip. Then she rested the mug on her leg and continued to scrutinize him.

"Do marvelous kisses always make you so crabby?" she finally asked.

His head snapped around, and he glared at her. "I shouldn't have kissed you. Even more, Miss Kane, *you* shouldn't have kissed *me*. Hell, you don't even know me from Adam. Do you always kiss men you've just met?"

"Only those I dump into snowdrifts," she said with a merry little laugh.

"Would you get serious?" he said, his voice rising.

"What is your problem? We shared a kiss, a wonderful kiss. You are, without a doubt, the most handsome man I've ever met, the kiss was fantastic, and that is that. End of story."

"Wrong. You're wrong, because I want to kiss you again . . . and again. I want to make love to you, too, right there on that rug in front of the fire. End of story? Not quite. This is just the first chapter, and you'd better give serious thought to what could happen in the

next one before you kiss me like that again."
He swore under his breath, then drained his
mug and set it on the tray with a dull thud.

"Is your sermonette over?" she asked pleasantly.

John-Trevor looked up at the ceiling and
groaned. "Give me strength."

"Would you like some more hot chocolate?"

"No."

"Oh." She paused. "Actually, you're getting
into an awful dither for no reason. I know
you . . . sort of. You're John-Trevor Payton,
you have brothers named Paul-Anthony and
James-Steven, you're half French. You're a
confirmed bachelor, you're gorgeous, and you
kiss like a dream. You have a good sense of
humor, as evidenced by the fact that you
didn't have me arrested for assault when I
plowed into you. You're—"

"Okay, okay," he said wearily, raising one
hand to silence her. "You've made your
point."

"As for the making love in front of the fire
part, you couldn't do that unless I agreed,
which I wouldn't because I'd have to be *in*
love before I *make* love. That's a firm rule of
mine, which by the way, most of the men I
date think is ridiculous. But . . ." She
shrugged.

John-Trevor turned to look at her again,
his eyes narrowed. "Are you saying that
you're a . . . that you've never . . ." He sliced
one hand through the air. "Cut. I'm not hav-

ing this conversation with you. I mean, cripes, people don't sit around talking about . . . Payton, shut up."

She laughed. "There's nothing embarrassing about the topic. Even after living here for five years, I'm still amazed at how uptight Americans are about"—she leaned toward him, her eyes comically wide, her voice dramatic—"you know, s-e-x."

She straightened and laughed. "I'm certainly not in a state of panic because I've never made love. I've had opportunities, and some of those men said they loved me, but I didn't love them." She shrugged. "It's fate, and if fate has it that I'm to fall in love with a man who loves me, then that's how it will be. I do hope it happens so I can have someone to share my life with. Oh, and a bushel of babies, of course."

"Of course," John-Trevor said, sounding weary again. "You're exhausting, Paisley, you really are. You're also the most delightfully refreshing woman I've ever had the pleasure of meeting."

"Thank you," she said, smiling at him warmly. "I like you, too, even if you do switch moods rather quickly. Do you live in Denver?"

"No, I'm from Los Angeles."

"I see. Well, that naturally leads to the next question, doesn't it?"

"What question?"

"Why are you here, John-Trevor?"

Two

Now they began, John-Trevor thought. The lies.

No, dammit, they weren't lies in the normal sense of the word. In his line of work, it was totally acceptable to do whatever was necessary—provided it was legal—to obtain information. The tricky part would be to make the "lies" sound plausible to someone as quick and curious as Paisley.

"John-Trevor?"

"What? Oh. Why am I here in Denver?" He leaned back and stretched his arms along the top of the sofa. "I own Payton Security. We do everything from providing bodyguards to finding missing people to installing security systems. You name it."

"How exciting," Paisley said, her eyes dancing. "So you're a private detective?"

He nodded. "I have my license."

"Do you carry a gun?"

"Rarely. I don't accept very many cloak-and-dagger assignments."

"What are you doing this time?" she asked, leaning toward him.

"I'm—I'm following up on some leads I have on the whereabouts of a guy who . . . who was the bookkeeper for a company in L.A. and took off with a hefty chunk of money. I've tracked him to Denver, but . . . It's not all that exciting, actually, nothing thrilling. What do *you* do for a living?"

"Wait, wait," she said, "Have you ever caught a crook red-handed?"

"Yes, but not lately. In the early days of Payton Security I took on just about any case that came along. Now I have a team of specialists who work for me, and the jobs are more sophisticated. Sometimes there's something unusual"— like now, like the assignment for Colonel Blackstone—"but for the most part it's pretty much run-of-the-mill. I took on the tracking down of this joker because I was ready for a break from paperwork."

"I still think it sounds exciting."

"It isn't," he said gruffly. "Where do *you* work?" Colonel Blackstone had only given him Paisley's name and address, wanting him, John-Trevor assumed, to have his own first impressions of her and her lifestyle. Considering the colonel's resources as a powerful and wealthy man, John-Trevor was certain he had gathered more information about his daughter than he'd shared. "Or do you just rent out rooms here for your cash flow?"

"Oh my, no," Paisley said. "I don't charge much for the rooms. Together, we make the mortgage payment and pay for utilities and food. I'm a translator for the library system. I make tapes of books—English into French, French into English."

"I'm impressed."

"It's no big deal. I was raised in Paris, remember? I spoke both languages from the time I could talk. I enjoy my work, though, very much. So many of the French novels bring back wonderful memories of my childhood. As much as I like Denver, there will always be a special place in my heart for Paris. Anyway, I'm being paid to read, which is one of my favorite pastimes. I'm one of those fortunate people who loves their job. Do you enjoy what you do?"

"Most of the time." But this assignment? John-Trevor thought. He was definitely experiencing mixed feelings. He was glad—*very* glad—he'd met the enchanting Miss Paisley Kane. But the knowledge that his report to Colonel Blackstone could have a tremendous effect on Paisley's life was starting to feel like a heavy weight on his shoulders.

Before Paisley could reply, they heard the front door open. A short, round woman who appeared to be in her late sixties entered the house. She carried a plastic tote bag covered in bright pink flamingos.

"It's bitter cold out," the woman said, "and the temperature is dropping fast. We're in for more snow. I got the makings for a salad, though, to go with the leftover stew from last night. That'll hit the spot. I—oh, you have company, Paisley."

"Gracie Smith meet John-Trevor Payton," Paisley said. "John-Trevor, this is Gracie. She lives here and does most of the cooking."

"Hello," John-Trevor said, starting to rise.

"Don't get up," Gracie said. She set the tote bag on the floor and removed her dark jacket, which she hung on the coat tree. "I'll be out of your way in a jiffy. I'm going to make the salad now."

John-Trevor blinked as the roly-poly woman disappeared down the hall.

"Interesting outfit," he said.

Paisley laughed. "Isn't she the cutest thing? I'm so used to what she wears, I don't even notice anymore. I guess fuchsia slacks and an orange sweatshirt is rather startling. She's one of the very rare women in the world who is color-blind, poor darling."

"Does she know her hair is bright blue?"

"I doubt it. She's always experimenting with hair coloring. I have no idea why. She's had green hair, purple hair, all kinds of colors. She seems to me to be totally color-blind—that is, blind to red, blue, *and* green."

"Where did you get her?"

"At the library. She doesn't have any family, and her apartment was condemned. She was quite literally out on the street. She spent the days at the library, then would sit in the bus station all night."

"So, you brought her here."

"Yes, about two years ago. She's a wonderful cook, which is a blessing for the rest of us, because I'm a disaster in the kitchen. My mother and I always ate in cafés and bistros." She said those two words with a definite French accent, which John-Trevor found as charming as the rest of her. "Maman's theory was that life was too short to spend it standing over a stove. Unusual for a French person, yes? I've tried to cook, but nothing ever turns out right."

"You make sensational hot chocolate," he said.

"Thank you."

Their eyes met, and the memory of the kiss they'd shared seemed to hover in the air between them, drawing them closer, although neither moved.

"John-Trevor," Paisley finally said, her voice unsteady, "you make me feel . . . so strange, so . . . I don't know what. I've known men in Paris, men here, but I've never met anyone like you."

John-Trevor lifted one hand and wove his fingers through her dark, silky curls.

"I've never met anyone like you, either,

Paisley," he said quietly. "You're a very rare, very special woman. I'm not the kind of man you should get mixed up with. I've been around the block too many times and . . . well, you're waiting for the guy who's going to give you that bushel of babies."

"Maybe I'm not meant to find him."

"I'm sure he'll come along."

"Fate has no master, John-Trevor."

"Sometimes we have to take charge of our own lives, *make* things happen." He shrugged. "I don't know. This is a little too metaphysical for me. I'm aware of what I want and don't want out of life. The rest of the time I just go with the flow, I guess. I suppose that's leaving some things to fate."

"Do you think it was fate that we met?"

He laughed. "Paisley, we met because you have a nutso inventor living under your roof. That wasn't fate. That was ridiculous."

"And the kiss?" she asked softly.

The kiss, he thought as he continued to sift her curls through his fingers. The kiss had been born of a longing, a need and want he'd never felt before. It had been heaven, and it had shaken him to the very depths of his being.

"Lust, babe," he said tersely, dropping his hand from her hair. He sat forward, resting his elbows on his knees as he stared into the fire. "Plain old lust."

Lust? Paisley repeated silently. What an awful thought. Such a crude word to describe something so incredibly . . . wondrous.

She stared at John-Trevor's profile, once again aware of his rough-hewn good looks, of how his thick fisherman's sweater emphasized his wide shoulders, of the power and virility that emanated from him. She remembered the taste of him, the scent of crisp winter air and man that had filled her senses, the heat that had radiated from his hard body and crept into hers.

She recalled his gentleness as he'd kissed her—and his raw desire.

Well, now, she mused, tapping one fingertip against her chin, this was rather confusing. John-Trevor Payton was certainly a complicated man. For some reason, he did not wish to acknowledge the emotional effect their kiss had had on him. He was dumping all of his reactions into the slot labeled "physical" and calling it lust.

But it had been more than that. She'd been the recipient of some kisses born of pure lust, and John-Trevor's kiss had possessed much more than that.

And if *she* knew it, then he knew it too. Yet he wasn't willing to admit it, maybe not even to himself. Confusing, but also very interesting.

"So," she said, "that was lust. Fascinating. I've often wondered what lust was like. You know, the urge to tear off one's clothes and jump into bed with someone. No feeling, no emotion, no caring, just a carnal want, a need for physical release. I certainly appreciate your explaining to me what that kiss was all about, John-Trevor. I have now experienced lust in its purest form." She batted her eyes at him. "My goodness, I'm really having adventures today. First my motor stuck, and now I've discovered lust."

"Dammit," he said, spinning on the sofa to face her, "would you cut it out? You keep saying 'lust' as if it were a new flavor of ice cream you tried. That kiss was more than that, Paisley. My wanting to make love to you was more than lust, too, for your information. So knock it off. Understand?"

She folded her hands primly in her lap and smiled at him. "Certainly. Whatever you say."

"Fine," he said, then shook his head. "What am I doing? What am I *saying*? You're driving me out of my tree, lady."

"Whatever you say," she murmured, still smiling.

"And quit saying 'whatever you say'!" he exclaimed.

"Okay. Whatever you—oops, I mean, sure, you bet. I won't say 'whatever you say' again. Those words will not pass my lips. I've stricken them from my vocabulary as of this moment. Poof . . . they're gone."

John-Trevor laughed.

He laughed because the other alternative was to put his fist through a wall to relieve his physical and mental frustration.

He laughed because Paisley had thrown him so off balance, he didn't know what to do with the amalgam of emotions churning within him.

He laughed because Paisley was a delightful, delectable, desirable woman, and he'd never, *ever* met anyone like her before.

He laughed, and it felt so damn good.

"Lord," he said finally, "I've totally lost it. You've pushed me over the edge of my sanity."

"You have a wonderful laugh," she said softly, almost to herself. "It's so rich and full. It would bring sunshine to the darkest day."

He looked at her in surprise, pleased by the compliment. "Well, I—ohmigod!" He stared at the doorway to the hall. "A cow. I just heard a cow. Do you rent a room to a homeless cow too?"

Paisley laughed as another extremely loud "Moo-o-o" reverberated through the air.

"That's one of the professor's inventions. It was going to be a whole set of doorbells that sounded like animals. No one was interested in investing in the project, though. So, he fiddled with the one he had—the cow—and installed it in the kitchen. It's Gracie's way of letting us know when a meal is ready. Will you join us for dinner? Gracie makes delicious stew."

"Thank you. That would be great."

"You can wash up in the bathroom off the kitchen."

He followed her down the hall to a large kitchen that ran along the back of the house. The white appliances, though far from new, were sparkling clean, and perky yellow-and-white-checked curtains hung on the windows. A rectangular wooden table with six ladder-back chairs stood at one end of the room.

The kitchen was pleasant, John-Trevor mused as he washed his hands in the small yellow-and-white bathroom. There was a homeyness about it that would urge people to linger over their meal and share the events of the day.

An image of his sleek, modern apartment in Los Angeles flashed through his mind. It was spacious and expensively decorated, yet compared to Paisley's home it was quiet and empty, lacking warmth.

When was the last time, he asked himself, that he'd laughed right out loud in his apartment? When, if ever, had he stepped over the threshold and felt a sense of welcoming comfort, as there was in Paisley's home? And when, in the name of heaven, had he given a moment's thought to sentimental junk like this?

"Moo-o-o!"

"Yeah, I'm coming, cow," he muttered, and reentered the kitchen.

His gaze immediately collided with the gaze of a young man who appeared to be seventeen or eighteen years old. His dark hair was shaggy and long, and though he was several inches shorter than John-Trevor, he was well-built. His brown eyes were cold, his gaze flickering over John-Trevor with the quick scrutiny of someone who was accustomed to measuring his opponent's worth.

This kid, John-Trevor thought, was street-wise. Judging from the size of his muscles, he probably pumped iron at least once a day. He was good-looking in a sulky, moody James Dean sort of way. He also, no doubt, lived there.

"Ah, you're back, John-Trevor," Paisley said. "This is Bobby Franklin. He lives here."

Of course, he did, John-Trevor thought dryly. Didn't everyone?

"Bobby," Paisley went on, "this is John-Trevor Payton. He's going to have dinner with us. I dumped him into a snowdrift when my motor stuck while I was testing the professor's skis."

"Just a temporary setback," the professor said, wringing his hands. "I'll have it corrected posthaste."

"We know you will, Professor," Paisley said, smiling at him. She redirected her attention to Bobby Franklin. "Bobby?"

"Yeah, right," he said, an edge to his voice. He extended his hand to John-Trevor. "Nice to meet you, Payton."

"John-Trevor or Mr. Payton," John-Trevor said, his own voice sharp.

He shook Bobby's hand, and the boy made a good attempt at crushing his fingers. He met Bobby's hostile gaze directly, and Bobby was the first to pull his hand free.

That boy, John-Trevor thought, was trouble. He had a chip on his shoulder a mile wide and looked as if he ate raw meat for breakfast. Why in the hell had Paisley brought a punk like that into her home? What a group.

"Here we go," she said, setting a tossed salad in a wooden bowl on the table. The stew was in a large casserole dish on a trivet. "Everyone dig in. John-Trevor, you can sit here. Professor, stop worrying about the motor and eat. Gracie, the stew smells delicious."

"Thank you, dear," Gracie said, adding a basket of bread to the table. "Bobby, you need a haircut."

"Yeah," Bobby said.

The dishes of food were passed around, then everyone gave serious attention to the meal.

This was the first time, Paisley thought suddenly, a spoonful of stew halfway to her mouth, that a man was sitting at the table at her invitation. Oh, they often had extra people for dinner, men included, who had dropped by to visit and simply stayed. But John-Trevor was a *man*, and he fell into a totally different category from the long-standing friends who often ate there.

Yes, she mused, John-Trevor Payton was most definitely a man. When he'd kissed her, she'd melted, just dissolved from the hot passion he'd aroused in her. For a moment she'd forgotten her vow to make love only with a man she loved. For a moment she'd wanted nothing more than for him to sweep her off to bed and love her until dawn. *Mon Dieu,* it was a good thing he'd stopped that kiss—but what would happen if he kissed her again?

And what, she wondered, allowing her thoughts free rein, would it be like to sit across the table from him at dinner every night? What would it be like to spend the evening with him, chatting, falling silent, glancing up to exchange warm smiles before returning to reading a book, or watching television? What would it be like to walk up the stairs with him, enter the bedroom, and make love in the four-poster where she now slept alone?

She looked at John-Trevor at the exact moment he shifted his gaze to her. A flush stained her cheeks as she had the irrational thought that he was peering into her brain, seeing the fanciful, sensual images there. She tore her gaze from his and turned to Bobby.

"How did work go today?" she asked.

" 'Kay," he mumbled around a bite of bread.

"Bobby is a top-notch mechanic," she said to John-Trevor. "He works at Chester's Garage and hasn't missed a day in over eleven months. Right, Bobby?"

"Yeah."

"Imagine that, Bobby. You've lived here nearly a year, Bobby."

"Yeah."

"Are there any more of you?" John-Trevor asked. "Or is this the whole . . . shall we say. . . family?"

Paisley smiled. "This is it. And 'family' is the perfect word for us. We just have each other."

Wrong, John-Trevor thought. Paisley had a father. A *very* wealthy father. Paisley Kane in diamonds and furs? He couldn't picture it. Well, it wasn't up to him to decide if Paisley should learn about her father. That decision rested on the colonel's shoulders. John-Trevor was just gathering the facts, ma'am.

He was also, he told himself firmly, going to keep his hands off Paisley Kane. But sweet heaven, that kiss had been something. Still, no matter how much he wanted to make love with her, it wasn't going to happen. Despite her ease in talking about "s-e-x," she was an innocent who was waiting for the man who would commit himself to her for life and give her "a bushel of babies." And that man was definitely *not* John-Trevor Payton.

"So, Bobby," he said, trying to banish the image of another man kissing her, loving her, "how did you become a member of Paisley's family?"

Bobby slowly lifted his head to frown at John-Trevor. "What's it to you?"

"Bobby," Gracie said, "don't be rude. John-Trevor is chatting, that's all."

"Yeah, right," Bobby said, still glaring at John-Trevor. "I met Paisley about a year ago when I was hot-wiring her car so I could steal it. My mom split when I was a kid, my dad disappeared a few years back. I ripped off stuff to get money to live. Satisfied . . . cop?"

"Bobby," Paisley said, "John-Trevor isn't a—"

"Oh, come on," Bobby said. "I can spot a cop a block away. Well, tough luck, fuzz, because I've been Mr. Clean for nearly a year. Hit on somebody else."

John-Trevor leaned back in his chair and crossed his arms over his chest. "You know something, Bobby? You've got an attitude problem. One of these days you're going to have that chip on your shoulder knocked off, and you'll be scraping yourself off the pavement."

"Yeah?" Bobby said. "And I suppose you're the guy who thinks he can do it. Anytime you're ready, cop, let me know. But when I whip your butt, you'll haul me in for assault. Right?"

Paisley opened her mouth to speak, then snapped it closed again, her gaze darting back and forth between John-Trevor and Bobby. Gracie, too, was gaping at the two. The professor appeared oblivious of the entire exchange.

John-Trevor shook his head in disgust.

"You're so off base, kid. I'm not a cop, but I'll give you credit for having a sharp eye. I'm a private detective. Private, Bobby, which means if I decide to take you apart, no one will know about it except you and me."

"John-Trevor, stop it," Paisley said. "Bobby, you too. You sound like little boys on the playground. Well, I won't have it, do you hear me? Not in my home. Am I making myself clear?"

"Yeah," Bobby said, and slouched over his plate again.

Paisley lifted her chin. "John-Trevor?"

Dandy, John-Trevor thought. He felt like a kid getting his hand slapped for misbehaving. However, considering the daggers in Miss Kane's dark eyes, he'd do well to shape up and shut up. Stupid, he wasn't.

He raised both hands in a gesture of peace. "Hey, no problem, Paisley. Bobby and I understand each other perfectly. We're going to be buddies. Right, Bobby?"

"Don't push it," Bobby muttered. "Paisley, there won't be any trouble, okay? Gracie, would you pass the bread? I like your hair this time, by the way."

"Oh?" Gracie patted her curls. "What color is it?"

"Blue," Bobby said. "*Very* blue."

"Oh, that's nice. I think I'd like blue. Not that I can ever really know, of course."

"Well, remember," Bobby said, "I'll tell you what color things are whenever you want.

But you know, Gracie, you've got it made. You can picture the colors in your mind any way you want them to be. The rest of us are stuck with red being red, green being green, that kind of jazz. There's no choice in the matter. But if someone says to you, 'your shirt is yellow,' you can imagine that color however you want it to be."

"Thank you, lovey," Gracie said, sniffling. "You always make me feel better about seeing the world only in shades of gray. Have some more stew."

John-Trevor glanced at Bobby in surprise and confusion. What a strange kid, he thought. One minute he was strutting his stuff like Mr. Slimeball, and the next he was exhibiting a sensitivity and gentleness toward an elderly lady.

He had decided that Bobby Franklin was a smart-mouthed, streetwise punk, nothing more. But Paisley, even though she had caught him trying to steal her car, must have seen beneath the surface of his tough facade. She was really something, all right.

"Listen to that wind pick up," she said. "It's going to be nasty out there tonight."

"Well, we're all snug as bugs right here," Gracie said. "There's no need for any of us to go out in this weather."

Her eyes wide, Paisley glanced at John-Trevor. He was smiling a very male, very now-what-sweetcakes? smile.

She sniffed indignantly. "Some of us, Gracie, don't live here."

"That's what sofas are for," Gracie said. "I think that's an ice storm out there. Listen to the noise at the windows. I'd bet my booties that's an ice storm. It won't be fit outside for man nor beast."

"Beast?" Bobby said, jumping to his feet. "Where's Maxine?"

"Quick," Paisley said. "Bobby, open the back door."

Bobby strode to the back door and flung it open, letting in a blast of frigid air, wet, stinging, icy rain, and a large, rather nondescript dog. She waddled into the room, shook herself vigorously, then wagged her tail.

"Maxine," Bobby said, "you're such a dope. Why didn't you whine, or scratch at the door?"

"She's a polite, ladylike dope," Paisley said. "Hi, Maxine. How are the babies? Goodness, she gets fatter every day. I think those puppies are due very soon."

Bobby filled a bowl with stew and set it on the floor. Maxine gobbled up the stew, her tail wagging the entire time. Bobby settled back down at the table.

"That's exactly what you need around here," John-Trevor said, chuckling. "Puppies."

"Well, she's obviously going to have some," Paisley said breezily. "Maxine showed up here one day about six or seven months ago and never left. Bobby named her Maxine."

"Why Maxine?" John-Trevor asked Bobby.

He shrugged. "I don't know. It fit. She looked like someone who smiles a lot, like a Maxine. She's really a great dog. Queen of ugly, but that's okay. I've never had a dog before."

John-Trevor glanced at the animal. "You're going to have a lot of dogs one of these days."

"I'll rewire the control box," the professor said, speaking for the first time during the meal. "Maybe I'll wax the bottom of the skis so there isn't such a drag on the motor. Yes, excellent. I must get back to work." He got up and hurried from the room.

"Bye, Professor," Paisley called after him. "Everyone ready for dessert? Gracie made an apple pie."

What a zoo, John-Trevor thought. If a person wasn't a fruitcake when he came into the house, he would be by the time he left. They were all nuts, they were weird . . . and they all cared about each other. They were a family.

And at the center of the circle of sunshine was Paisley.

Delightful Paisley Kane. . . .

Three

Everyone, except the absent professor, pitched in to clean up the kitchen after consuming huge slices of scrumptious apple pie.

At least, John-Trevor mused as he put the butter away, Bobby seemed to have declared an uneasy truce. While the kid wasn't noticeably rude, neither did Bobby speak to him, nor even acknowledge his presence.

The moment that the kitchen was set to rights, Bobby disappeared up the stairs, with a tail-wagging Maxine lumbering behind him. Gracie said it was time for her favorite television program and went upstairs too.

John-Trevor volunteered to add logs to the fire in the living room. Paisley agreed, and leaping flames soon sent a warm glow over the entire room. Paisley sat on the sofa, while John-Trevor remained by the fire, leaning one arm on the mantel and gazing at her.

He had to play this exactly right, he told himself. The scene had been set by talk of the worsening weather over dinner. Plus, sweet, old, blue-haired Gracie had calmly announced that the sofa was an understood place for a person to sleep, rather than letting him venture out into a horrendous storm.

Spending the night in Paisley's home, John-Trevor deduced, would afford him the opportunity to gather more data. And be close to her for hours, see her smile, hear her laughter, enjoy the very essence of her lively, refreshing personality. And maybe, just maybe, he'd have the chance to take her in his arms and kiss her again, hold her, savor her . . .

Come on, Payton, he admonished himself. He was supposed to be doing the job he'd been hired for, nothing more. He would put together a clear picture of Paisley's life, hightail it out of there, report to Colonel Blackstone, then head for home.

Again the image of his large apartment flashed before his eyes. And again he saw it as empty, cold, offering no welcome. He pushed the unsettling scene from his mind.

"The fire is lovely," Paisley said, bringing John-Trevor from his tangled thoughts. "The flames are hypnotizing. My mind keeps drifting off in a dozen directions."

"Such as?" he asked. "What do you think

about when you fall under the spell of the fire?"

She smiled up at him, then redirected her attention to the crackling flames. "Everything. Nothing. My thoughts bounce around like a rubber ball. I pretend I can buy Bobby his own garage, where he'll be the best mechanic in the state. And I have the professor invent something so amazing, he'll be famous. I see a marvelous kitchen for Gracie, with sparkling new appliances and every fancy gadget ever made."

"What about you, Paisley? Don't you daydream about what *you* want?"

She shrugged. "I have all I need, John-Trevor."

"What about that special man and your bushel of babies?"

"That's up to fate. Fantasizing isn't going to make him appear. My stained-glass dream rainbow won't bring him to me, either. I rest gently on the dream of loving and being loved, because it might never happen." She shrugged in typical French fashion and continued to gaze into the fire.

" 'Rest gently on a dream'?" John-Trevor repeated. "That's an unusual expression. I've never heard it before. What does it mean?"

"Well . . ." Paisley started, then stopped.

Only a handful of people, she mused, knew the meaning, the importance, of her mother's stained-glass panel. It was so special, so private, she was never quick to tell its story.

Yet for some unknown reason, she wanted John-Trevor to know, wanted to share it with him. It was as though it would be wrong *not* to.

She lifted her head to meet his gaze. A wistful smile touched her lips.

"To rest gently on dreams," she said quietly, "is something my mother taught me from the time I was very small. She called that stained-glass panel her rainbow of dreams. Each different-colored diamond represented a secret dream that she never shared, not even with me."

"Go on," John-Trevor urged, his gaze riveted on her.

"My mother told me that dreams were as fragile as that pretty glass. She said that it was fine to escape from reality for a short time and dwell on dreams, but one should never rely on them for happiness. 'Rest gently on dreams, Paisley,' she always said, 'so that they don't shatter and will be there for another time.' "

She paused, gazing at the fire again, then looked back at John-Trevor.

"So, yes, I touch the stained glass when I come home to say a hello, of sorts, to my mother, but I rest gently on it because it's *my* dream rainbow now."

A sudden ache tightened John-Trevor's throat. Although he wasn't a man who ever cried, he realized tears were building behind his eyes. That was ridiculous. Just because

Paisley had told him the tale about her mother's stained glass; just because she had spoken of the fragility of dreams in such a soft voice, with such emotion in her eyes, that he wanted to make every one of her dreams come true . . .

He roughly cleared his throat. "That was a lovely story," he said. "Rest gently on dreams." He nodded. "That's good advice. I know people who rely on their dreams to get them from one day to the next, because they don't have the fortitude to face reality. Dreams weren't meant to be used that way. Rest gently on dreams . . . Your mother was very wise, Paisley."

"I know." Her eyes turned misty, as though she were suddenly swept away on a sea of memories. She blinked, then took a deep breath. "So! Tell me about this man you're looking for."

What man? he thought hazily. Oh, hell, the guy he'd invented as an excuse to be in Denver. He'd forgotten all about that nonsense.

"What does he look like?" she asked. "If I had a description of him, I could keep my eyes open for him. This is exciting. Now, don't fret that I'll do anything foolish like trying to make a citizen's arrest if I see him. I'll report directly to you. Is he tall, short, fat, skinny, what?"

Damned if he knew, John-Trevor thought. "He's a twit. You know, short, thin, going bald. He's in his forties, wears thick glasses, has buck teeth, and wears plaid pants a lot. The guy is really into plaid pants."

"He doesn't sound like a very villainous villain. That's rather disappointing. But a crook is a crook, and it's still exciting. What else should I know?"

"He has hay fever," John-Trevor said, getting on a roll. "Summer, winter, it doesn't matter, the creep always has a handkerchief in his hand, blowing his nose, dabbing at his eyes. Very bad hay fever."

"Maybe he took the money so he could travel the world until he found a doctor to cure his hay fever," Paisley said, her eyes sparkling. "He was desperate, couldn't bear one more day of a runny nose. Poor little man. But the fact remains that he stole the money. I'll be on the alert for him, John-Trevor."

"That's very comforting," he said, chuckling.

His smile faded as he continued to look directly into Paisley's big, dark eyes. Without realizing he'd done it, he started toward her. In the next instant he stopped dead in his tracks as the professor rushed into the room.

"Paisley, Paisley, excuse me," the professor said. He picked up one of her feet, peered at the bottom of her shoe, then nodded and dropped her foot. "Mmm. Thank you."

"You're welcome," Paisley said pleasantly.

The professor hurried away, muttering

under his breath. John-Trevor shook his head and sat down on the sofa next to her.

"Your professor is nuts," he said.

"Dedicated, not nuts," she said firmly. "There are a great many people in this world who just sit back and wait for things to be handed to them, as though life owes them material possessions. The professor is working very hard toward his goals. I admire and respect that."

"You've got a point there. He certainly gives it his all. I've met my share of those who stand around with their hands out, waiting for someone to pick up the tab."

"So have I. My mother always said that we might not have much, but what was ours had been earned by honest, hard work and that was something to be proud of."

"Your mother sounds great. I wish I could have met her." He paused. "Paisley, what about your father? You never talk about him."

"I don't know who he is. My mother wouldn't tell me his name. She never married, simply refused to give up her independence to a man. She said my father was wonderful, a kind, caring, handsome man, and she loved him very much. Things were rather strained between them when they parted, though. My father was enormously wealthy and felt he could convince my mother to marry him because of his money. She told me over and over never to be blinded by wealth, to be certain I didn't get swept away by what was offered to me and forget to stay true to myself."

"I see," John-Trevor said.

"If it hadn't been for my father's money, maybe my mother would have . . . Well, I really don't know. I do know that he was the only man she ever loved, and he gave her her two most precious gifts. Me, and the stained-glass panel."

"Don't you . . . well, sort of resent the fact that she wouldn't tell you who he was?"

" 'Resent' is too strong a word, John-Trevor. I've often *wished* I could see my father, if even from a distance, just so I would know what he looked like, instead of having shifting and changing images of him in my imagination. He wasn't a young man when he knew my mother. He was about fifty then, she said. I've drawn hundreds of pictures of him in my mind, but . . ." She shook her head. "That's so foolish. I was created in love, John-Trevor, and that's going to have to be enough for me to know, because I'll never have more than that. In fact, it's better this way."

"Why?"

"Well, if he's still very wealthy, he might try to buy my affections, like he did with my mother. He didn't mean to hurt her, but he did, and there's no guarantee he learned any lesson from it. My daydreams about him are safer by far than actually knowing who he is."

Plain enough, John-Trevor thought. Hell, what a mess. Her father was a rich, lonely old man who had the financial means to grant Paisley's every dream. And Paisley could add a burst of sunshine and laughter to Colonel Blackstone's final years. What would the colonel do, what decision would he reach about revealing who he was to his daughter?

"Well, I'd better hit the road," John-Trevor said. "The car I rented is going to be a solid block of ice if I don't move it. I left it a mile or so from here." Play it cool, Payton. Easy does it. "Is there anything special I should know about driving in this kind of weather? Being from California, I'm out of my element here." Nice touch. This was where Paisley would insist that he sleep on the sofa. Lord, he was sharp.

She frowned. "An ice storm is nothing to fool around with, John-Trevor. It's not like a pretty snowfall. I think . . ."

"Yes?" he asked, raising his eyebrows in pure innocence.

". . .That you should call a taxi to take you to your hotel. Then you won't have to attempt to drive in this weather."

"A taxi," he echoed. "Right." Talk about striking out at the plate. "May I use your phone?"

"Of course. There's one in the kitchen."

A few minutes later, he returned to the living room and sat back down on the sofa.

"It'll be about forty-five minutes," he said. "A lot of people are taking taxis tonight, I guess."

Hooray! Paisley thought. She didn't want him to leave, not yet. The very idea of his walking out the door made her feel strangely empty and cold inside. She didn't know why. All she was certain of was that she wanted John-Trevor there, in her home, for a little bit longer.

"Well, good, because we can talk some more," she said, smiling brightly. "Tell me all about your brothers, what the three of you did when you were little boys, everything."

John-Trevor frowned in confusion. "Why?"

"Because I just met you, and I want to know all about you."

"Why?"

"My mother used to tell me that some people spend all their time wishing they led a more exciting life. They complain that they don't have the opportunity to travel, to have adventures. 'They're so foolish, Paisley,' she would say to me. 'Don't they realize that every new person they meet is an adventure, a wonderful source of experience, of learning things they didn't know before?' She greeted each day with anticipation of the people who would cross her path. She'd say, 'Life is people, people are life.' "

"As I said before, your mother was quite a

woman," John-Trevor said quietly. "You must miss her very much."

"Yes, I do. I was barely nineteen when she died, and I didn't see how I could handle living without her. But I soon realized I had strengths I didn't know I possessed, because she'd seen to it that I did. Yes, I still miss her, but I have many wonderful memories of her."

"Why did you move to Denver? From Paris, France, to Denver, Colorado, is quite a jump."

"My mother left me this house in her will. I didn't even know she owned it. There was a stipulation that I couldn't receive the deed unless I actually came here and saw it. Then I could stay or sell it, whichever I wanted."

"I wonder why she did that," John-Trevor said idly.

"At first," Paisley said, "my imagination went wild, and I thought there was a secret purpose to my coming to Denver. But as time passed, I decided that was silly. My mother simply wanted me to have the opportunity to live in her native country, which I'd never seen."

"And you stayed."

She nodded. "I came in the spring when the flowers were in bloom, and it was so beautiful. I loved this house from the moment I walked in the door. One of the first things I did was to have the stained-glass panel installed. We had moved so often in

Paris, because my mother loved the challenge of fixing up a new place, meeting new people. It's not easy to find apartments in Paris, but my mother knew so many people, and always seemed to be hearing about one that was coming available in Montmartre or Montparnasse or on the Left Bank. I suppose it was exciting, but sometimes it was difficult for me, and . . . Anyway, I knew when I came here that I wanted a sense of security, of knowing I could stay as long as I wanted to."

"Are you happy, Paisley?"

"Yes, of course I'm happy."

"No, wait," he said, raising one hand. "Don't answer so quickly, so automatically."

"There's no other way to answer, John-Trevor. I am who I am, my life is what it is." She shrugged. "So, I'm happy."

"Okay, fine, but what if your life changed drastically all of a sudden? What if . . . Oh, let's see here. Try this one. What if you won the lottery, you know, millions of dollars? This isn't a one-shot deal of buying Bobby a garage or getting Gracie a deluxe food processor. I'm talking about an entirely different life-style. You wouldn't have to work. You could own a big mansion, designer clothes, furs, jewelry. You could travel anywhere in the world whenever the whim hit. No stress, no strain, no worries. Do you think you'd be happy living a life like that?"

She laughed. "Probably not. Then I'd have to hobnob with people who called one another 'darling' all the time. I don't think I could handle that."

"I'm serious, Paisley."

"Well, goodness, John-Trevor, my imagination can only stretch so far. The life-style you're describing is beyond my scope. I learned from my mother to be content with what I've worked to obtain. Let's talk about reality. Tell me all about yourself."

Dammit, John-Trevor thought. He *was* discussing reality.

"Why are you so adamant about never marrying?" she asked abruptly.

He opened his mouth, but couldn't think of what to say. "Where did that come from?"

"We're talking about you now, remember? You know all about me, so it's my turn to ask about you." She cocked her head as she looked at him. "You never want to marry because you're so gorgeous, you can change women as easily as you do your shirt, right?" She laughed. "I love American clichés. They're so appropriate sometimes."

John-Trevor felt an unnatural heat creep up his neck. "For Pete's sake, Paisley. I'm not going to talk about other women with you."

"Surely you realize that you're as handsome as . . . as the day is long." She frowned. "That's one cliché I don't quite understand. Anyhow," she continued brightly, "I'm sure you've met enough women who—"

"Would you cut it out?" he interrupted in frustration. "I don't want to get married because it's a tremendous undertaking, makes you responsible for the welfare and happiness of another person. I'd rather go about my business answering only to myself, thank you. Besides that, I would be a sitting duck emotionally for whatever shot that person pulled on me. Nope. No way. Not me."

"But what if you fall in love?"

"I don't intend to . . . ever. Okay? End of discussion?"

She leaned toward him. "John-Trevor, you're forgetting about fate. If you are meant to fall in love, you won't have any say in the matter. If fate decrees it, there you'll be"—she snapped her fingers—"smack-dab in love, a goner."

"Not a chance," he said gruffly.

She sat back, crossed her arms, and smiled.

John-Trevor glared at her. "What's that funny little smile for?" He narrowed his eyes. "Look, if I decide—which I have—never to fall in love, never to marry, then that's how it's going to be. Got that?"

"Whatever you say, John-Trevor."

He groaned and rolled his eyes heavenward. "You're exasperating as hell, you know."

She pressed one hand over her heart. "*Moi?*"

"Oh, no, you don't. You're not going to start whipping a bunch of French on me. It's hard enough to carry on a sane conversation with you in English."

She laughed, and the heat of desire burst within John-Trevor once more. Lord above, he thought, this woman was driving him nuts. And she was causing him to ache with a need so intense, it would drive a saint to drink. She'd thrown him so off kilter, he felt like a gawky teenager who didn't know what to do with his hands.

He strode across the room and hunkered down in front of the fireplace. After yanking open the screen, he began jabbing at the blazing logs with a poker.

Paisley watched him, hoping he didn't hear the sigh that escaped from deep within her. Fascinated, she stared at his strong hand as he wielded the poker, and a longing to feel that hand stroke her hair, caress her skin, began to build inside her. Struggling to control her wayward libido, she tore her gaze from his hand—only to have it fall on his tight buttocks and solid thighs, displayed to great advantage by his well-worn jeans. Thankfully, he distracted her by shifting to reach for another log, but then her breath caught as the firelight enhanced the lean, hard planes of his face.

He was beautiful, she mused, and it felt so . . . so right to have him in her home. It suddenly seemed as though something had been missing in the house, in her life, and now all was complete because John-Trevor was with her.

Oh, Paisley, don't, she admonished herself. From the time she'd been old enough to understand, she'd listened carefully as her mother urged her to leave matters of the heart to fate.

Well, Paisley mentally argued, hadn't it been fate's hand that had caused her motor to get stuck, then propelled her into John-Trevor? The timing had been perfect, surely preordained by fate itself.

Except . . .

Except John-Trevor wanted no part of love, commitment, marriage, babies. Fate was obviously flawed on occasion. Now, she decided, fate needed a nudge. She was going to step in and take charge because she deserved to know if John-Trevor was the man destined to be hers for all time.

He finished fiddling with the fire and sat down on the sofa again.

"So," she said, "tomorrow is Sunday. I hope we're not snowed in, or iced in. There's so much to see and do in Denver, and Sunday is my day for exploring. Would you like to go around with me? Providing, of course, the weather isn't too grim."

He felt, John-Trevor mused, like a man standing on the edge of what he knew was a pool of quicksand, and he was dumb enough to be considering actually taking a step into it. Paisley was doing tricky things to his mind and body, and he should put a great deal of distance between himself and her very quickly.

But he couldn't, he reasoned, because he had a job to do for Colonel Blackstone. There was more data to be gathered, facts to piece together to get a clearer picture of what made Paisley tick. So, he'd spend the day with her. All in the line of duty, of course.

"Sure, I'll explore Denver with you tomorrow, Paisley," he said, turning his head to look at her. "You can be my tour guide. If I freeze to death out there, though, I'll hold you responsible."

"Fair enough," she said, smiling.

He studied her for a moment, then asked, "Do you have a secret dream for each of the sections of the stained glass?"

"No," she said. "I give a great deal of careful thought to those dreams. There are very few of them assigned to the different diamonds."

"And you rest gently on those that are there."

"Yes."

"Do you think that all of your mother's dreams came true?"

"I don't know, because she never told me what they were."

"Or who your father was."

Paisley frowned. "John-Trevor, does it disturb you that my mother never married my father, that I was born without the benefit of his name?"

"Lord, no. I'm not standing in judgment, Paisley. I guess it's because I've been doing the kind of work I'm in for so many years. I'm a detective, I solve mysteries, puzzles. Unanswered questions bother me. I could help you, you know, discover who your father is."

"Thank you, but no. After all these years I . . . No."

"Okay, but consider this. That man has a daughter, a delightful young woman, whom he had a part in creating. What about respecting *his* right to know that you exist?"

"John-Trevor, we're talking about something that took place nearly twenty-five years ago. My father has probably forgotten he ever knew Kandi Kane. He's no doubt married, has a family of his own."

"But what if he isn't? What if he's alone? What if he never forgot Kandi Kane and his love for her? What if your existence, your emergence into his life, could mean tremendous joy for him? Did you ever think about that?"

Paisley's frown returned, and she stared at John-Trevor for a long moment before speaking again.

"You're making it sound," she said finally, "as though I'm selfishly shirking my responsibilities, as if I *owe* it to this man to find him and tell him he has a daughter."

"Well, no, that's not what I mean. You're not at fault here in any way. I was just pre-

senting the flip side of the coin, that's all."
What he was actually doing, he thought, was
blowing this so badly it was a crime. He was
putting Paisley on the defensive about knowing who her father was, which would bring
Colonel Blackstone to the plate with two
strikes against him. Damn. "Forget I men-
tioned it. I was only talking."

"Oh." She sat silent for a minute, her lips
pursed in a moue. "You know, I never gave a
moment's thought to the other side of the
coin, as you put it. I accepted my mother's
decision as being the way things were and
got on with my life. Now I feel as though . . .
as though my father has taken center stage,
announcing that it's time that his needs and
rights were taken into consideration. This is
all rather confusing."

"Hey, just put it away for now," John-
Trevor said. "I didn't mean to upset you.
Don't think about it any more tonight.
Okay?"

She didn't respond, but simply stared off
into space.

"Paisley? Come on, don't dwell on this."

"What?" She met his gaze. "Well, it is food
for thought. I— Oh, there's your taxi. I hear
the horn honking."

They both stood, and Paisley walked with
him to the door. John-Trevor shrugged into
his coat, then slid one hand to the nape of
her neck. He captured her mouth in a searing kiss that left them both breathless.

"Noon? Tomorrow?" he said, close to her lips.

"Fine. Yes," she whispered. "Good night, John-Trevor."

He left the house, and Paisley stood perfectly still, staring at the stained-glass panel in the door.

Four

Hours later, John-Trevor lay on the king-size bed in his hotel room, staring up into the darkness. He'd tossed and turned until his muscles ached with tension, and he was still, he knew, a long way from falling asleep.

The bed was as comfortable as any hotel bed was capable of being. He was finally warm again, well-fed, and should be snoozing like a baby. Instead, he was wired and unable to quiet the cacophony in his mind. And it was all Paisley's fault.

Her image danced in his mind with such crystal clarity, it was as if she were standing before him, her smile lighting up her face, her dark eyes sparkling. He could hear her wind-chime laughter, smell her special aroma of fresh air and flowers, and still taste the sweet nectar of her lips.

With a groan, he rolled over again. The need to mesh his body with hers, to become one with her, had increased a hundredfold since he'd kissed her good night. But it was not just his physical desire for Paisley that was keeping the blessed oblivion of sleep at bay. Foreign and disturbing emotions were also chipping away at his peace of mind.

He felt oddly protective of her, wanting to stand between her and anything, or anyone, who might harm her. Possessiveness, too, was rearing its unfamiliar head, bringing with it anger at the thought of any man other than himself touching her, holding and kissing her.

And right in the middle of the mess called his mind was the ever-present reminder of why he was really there. The assignment for Colonel Blackstone.

"Hell," he muttered.

After a few more muttered expletives, he closed his eyes and gratefully gave way to the somnolence that claimed him.

Paisley slowly opened her eyes to find sunlight filling her bedroom. She stretched contentedly, then excitement tingled through her as she remembered the previous evening. In just a few hours, she would see John-Trevor again, and they would spend the afternoon together. It would be glorious. She hoped.

Paisley sat up and told herself not to get

carried away. Maybe fate had brought them together, but that did not mean that they were meant for each other, or that he'd change his mind about marriage.

On the other hand, she mused, he *could* be *the* man. After all, in all the years she'd dated, no boy or man had ever aroused in her much more than friendly interest and a vague sexual excitement. Comparing her feelings toward those erstwhile boyfriends with her feelings toward John-Trevor was like comparing a mere fireworks display with a supernova. *Mon Dieu*, what that man did to her when he touched her. . . .

Enough! Paisley thought. If she spent the entire morning chasing her thoughts around like this, she'd be exhausted by the time John-Trevor arrived.

Tossing back the covers, she slipped out of bed and crossed the room to the window. The sky was clear and the sun was shining, its warmth rapidly melting the ice from last night's storm.

It was going to be a beautiful day in Denver, she thought, and she was spending it with John-Trevor Payton.

She showered and washed her hair, then dressed in winter-white slacks and sweater. She twisted two chiffon scarves together, one pale pink, the other a shade darker, and tied them loosely around her neck so that they fell in a frothy burst of color over the front of the sweater.

Her makeup was light, as always, but was the perfect blend of blush, highlighter, shadow, and lipstick to enhance her skin and eyes. She applied the cosmetics with expertise, absently remembering how her mother had taught her when she was a teenager to enhance her looks subtly.

Downstairs, she stopped and looked at the stained-glass panel. Sunlight poured through the colored diamonds, casting enchanting rainbows on the walls and floor.

Did she dare, she wondered, place herself and John-Trevor as a couple, as two becoming one, in a section of the panel? No, no, she mustn't. Not yet, maybe never. For even if she rested gently on that dream, it was so special, so important, that if she was wrong, she'd end up with a shattered heart.

"Oh, Maman," she whispered, "life is so confusing at times."

John-Trevor strode up the front walk to Paisley's house, then slowed as he reached the porch.

With any luck, he mused, Bobby, Gracie, and the professor would be off somewhere, doing whatever they did on a Sunday afternoon. He wanted, he *needed*, to pull Paisley into his arms and kiss her the moment he saw her. It had been his first thought upon awakening and had grown in intensity ever since.

Get practical, Payton, he told himself. This outing was also professionally important. The plan of exploring Denver with Paisley suited his purpose just fine. He intended to probe deeper, discover more about her life, what she might be lacking on a material level, what secret dreams she might have that seemed out of her reach due to her present financial status.

But all of that didn't mean he couldn't kiss her. Just one more time.

He pressed the doorbell, then blinked in surprise when he heard the first bars of "Here Comes Peter Cottontail." Bobby opened the door a moment later.

So much for luck, John-Trevor thought. "Hi, kid."

"Yeah," Bobby said. "So come in, I suppose."

John-Trevor stepped into the front hall and unbuttoned his sheepskin jacket. "Don't knock yourself out," he said, matching Bobby's glare. "Did that doorbell play 'Here Comes Peter Cottontail'?"

"Yeah, the professor invented it. Well, he thought he did, but then he found out there were already musical doorbells, so he quit after the rabbit bit."

"Oh. How's he doing with the skis?"

"Not so hot. He decided to wax the bottom of the things and got some beeswax from a guy, but it was gummed up with honey and the skis are really a sticky mess now."

John-Trevor smiled and shook his head. "He's something, that professor. Where's Gracie?"

"She's getting ready to go play bingo. She's nuts about bingo. I picked her clothes so she'd look good. Blue sweater, blue slacks. They match her hair, so she's color coordinated from head to toe."

John-Trevor's smile shifted to a serious expression. "You're a nice guy when you decide you want to be, Bobby. Why do you waste so much time and energy with the tough-hood routine?"

"Don't push me, Payton," Bobby said, narrowing his eyes, "and listen up to this too. If you hurt Paisley, I'm coming after you. You may be bigger than I am, but you'll know I've been all over you."

"I have no intention of hurting Paisley."

"Says you. She's been acting weird last night and this morning. Like she has a special secret. And she smiles when there's nothing to smile about. Her eyes keep getting all big and dreamy, like she's high on something. I don't know what's going on between you two, but if you upset her I'll—"

"Hello," Paisley said, emerging from the kitchen at the end of the hall. *Oh, hello, John-Trevor,* she thought as she walked toward him. In a dark green sweater and gray slacks, he was scrumptious. And she was so very, very glad he was there. "Are you two having a nice chat?" she asked, looking at Bobby, then John-Trevor.

"Charming," John-Trevor said. "You look lovely, Paisley. Are you ready to go?"

"Yes. I just need my coat," She pointed to a long dark-burgundy coat hanging on the brass tree.

John-Trevor assisted her with the coat, then reached for the doorknob.

"Have a good time at the gym, Bobby," Paisley said. "You're going, aren't you? Like you do every Sunday?"

"Yeah," Bobby said. "Remember what I said, Payton."

John-Trevor decided to ignore Bobby's parting shot and left the house with Paisley.

"What did Bobby mean by that?" she asked as they walked to his car.

"He's just throwing his muscle around," he said. "He thinks he's your keeper, or body-guard."

"Oh, I see. Well, he's protective of me like a brother would be. We're all a family, you know, and he feels he has certain responsi-bilities. Please be patient with him."

"No problem."

We're all a family, John-Trevor thought as Paisley directed him to the downtown area. That was just dandy, but the family had an unknown member waiting in the wings. Paisley's father.

And what, he wondered as he stopped at a red light, had Bobby meant about Paisley's acting strangely? She wasn't . . . falling in love with him, was she? That would be wonderful, fantastic—no, dammit, that would be terrible. Ah, hell, he couldn't think straight.

He forced his jumbled thoughts to the back of his mind and concentrated on his driving and the city. Denver was an intriguing blend of old and new. Mirror-windowed skyscrapers rose alongside Victorian-era buildings that had been restored to preserve the history of the old West.

"This is a fascinating city," he said.

"Oh, I know," Paisley said. "We should go to the Brown Hotel. It's marvelous. It was built in 1892, during the mining days when Denver was booming. Would you like to look at some art also?"

"Sure."

"There's a wonderful collection in the Museum of Western Art in the Navarre building that includes works by Frederic Remington and Georgia O'Keeffe. Do you want to go there first?"

"You're the boss," he said, smiling over at her quickly. "Your wish is my command today."

"Well, how nice. I feel very pampered."

Perfect line, John-Trevor thought. "You deserve to be pampered. I can picture you living a life of ease, having all those mundane everyday chores taken care of for you. That would leave you free to—to . . . um, do whatever it is you'd like to do."

"Turn right at the next corner, go two blocks, then turn left," she said. "What does one do when one is not required to tend to mundane chores?"

"Beats me." He blinked. "No, that's the wrong answer," he added quickly. "You could pursue all kinds of things you've never had time for before. You could . . . learn to knit."

"I know how to knit."

"Oh." He frowned. "Well, hell, Paisley, I don't know. There's a whole slew of rich, pampered women in this world who manage to fill their days. I think they do a lot of volunteer work. That's it. They help those less fortunate than themselves."

"I already do volunteer work. I make story tapes for the blind so they can enjoy books as much as people who can see. Why are we discussing all this?"

"Why? Why. Well, because I . . . because from what I've seen, you give a great deal to others. You know, Gracie, the professor, charming Bobby. What's missing is the spotlight's being focused on you, your having the opportunity to live a full, exciting, adventuresome life. You like Paris. So, you have a house in Paris, a fancy place here in Denver, maybe—maybe a beachfront place in, say, California."

She wrinkled her nose. "That doesn't appeal to me. I'd feel like a visitor who had dropped by. I told you, I like my sense of permanence here because I moved so often as a child. And I'm perfectly happy with my house. I wouldn't change a thing for the world."

"Now wait, don't be so hasty. You like animals. Maxine is no prize specimen, but you still gave her a home. How about a ranch? You could raise horses or pigs or whatever."

She laughed. "That's ridiculous. As for Maxine, I gave her a home because she didn't have one. I like animals, but not to the point that I'd want to live on a ranch and raise pigs, for heaven's sake. John-Trevor, I realize we're playing 'let's pretend' or something, but turn it around for a minute. What if *you* suddenly became very wealthy. Would you give up your job, chuck the company you've worked so hard to make successful? What would *you* do with yourself all day?"

"Well, I'd . . . well . . ."

"You'd be bored to death."

"Right," he said, frowning. "I would."

"I rest my case."

"You *can't* rest your case. You have to think about . . . Forget it."

She laughed. "Good idea. Pull into that parking lot up ahead on the right."

An hour later, John-Trevor was completely frustrated. He stood next to Paisley, pretending to study the painting on the wall, and trying not to frown.

For the life of him, he couldn't get her to give more than a fleeting thought to what her life could be like if she were wealthy. It was becoming very clear that while Kandi had eventually forgiven Colonel Blackstone for his conduct, the damage had been done. Paisley's unbending attitude toward money, whether she knew it or not, was a product of Kandi's hurt. He was *not* doing well with his assignment at the moment.

"Hey," he said, shifting his gaze, "isn't that painting over there a scene in Paris? This may be a western-art museum, but I'd swear that's Paris."

They moved several feet to stand in front of the painting.

"Oh, yes, it *is* Paris," Paisley said, smiling with pleasure and excitement. "I know that street, John-Trevor. See the little outdoor café? I can't tell you how many times I ate there with my mother and her friends when I was a little girl." Her smile turned puckish. "I *can* tell you how spoiled I was though, Maman's friends always treating me as though I were the future queen of England. Most of them, you see, didn't have children of their own; so they spoiled me to their heart's content, then gave me back to Maman to deal with."

She laughed, and John-Trevor smiled, picturing a lively little dark-haired, dark-eyed girl playing in the gardens of Paris.

"It sounds as though you had a great childhood," he said.

"Oh, yes. The best."

"You know, Paisley, there's a definite longing in your voice when you speak of Paris. I think you miss it more than you realize. You said you like your sense of permanence here, but Paris is so much a part of who you are, I believe you could move back and forth between here and there and still feel settled in, like you belong."

"Maybe," she said thoughtfully. "But there's no sense in dwelling on it." She turned around and looked up at him. "I don't exactly have a budget that includes jet-setting between Denver and Paris."

"Well, suppose that—"

Her eyes suddenly widened, and she grabbed the lapels of his jacket. "Shh. Don't move. Act naturally. Oh, my gosh."

"What's the matter?"

"It's him," she whispered. "The crook in the plaid pants."

"Huh?"

"The man you're after, John-Trevor. He's across the room looking at a Remington. Yes, yes, it's him. Plaid pants, buck teeth, and he's blowing his nose, though no glasses. Do you think he used some of the money for contact lenses?"

"Good Lord," John-Trevor said, rolling his eyes. "I can't believe this."

"Let's shift somehow so you can see him. We mustn't be obvious about it, though. Remember, act naturally."

"You're the boss."

And with that, he lifted her off her feet,

swung her around, set her back down, and
kissed her. Paisley stared in shock for a
moment, then sighed and closed her eyes.

The instant his lips touched Paisley's,
John-Trevor knew he'd made a mistake. He
hadn't intended to kiss her in the middle of
a museum, but now that he was, he never
wanted to stop. Her lips parted, her tongue
met his, and he was lost as a tidal wave of
heated desire swept through him with raging
force.

The insistent voice that warned him he
shouldn't be doing this was silenced, and a
single thought exploded in his mind. *Paisley
Kane was his!* He groaned silently and deepened the kiss, tightening his arms around
her.

She slid her hands to his neck, her fingers
tangling in his thick hair. Beneath the
urgent, hungry onslaught of his mouth, she
gave herself completely, with total abandon.
It was so wonderful, and so right. Fate had
seen to it that she would find John-Trevor by
dumping him into a snowdrift. But now she
was positive fate *did* need a helping hand.
The rest would be up to her.

With great effort, John-Trevor finally tore
his mouth from hers. "Dear Lord," he muttered. "We've got to stop. This isn't the time,
or the place."

"What?" she asked dreamily, slowly opening her eyes. "Oh!" she exclaimed, totally

emerging from her sensual fog. "I told you to act naturally."

He grinned. "I did."

"Mmm." She tried to look stern, but failed completely. "Is it him? The plaid-pants crook?"

"Nope. You have a sharp eye, but it's not him. That guy over there is too tall, too young, too heavy."

"Well, darn."

John-Trevor chuckled. "Let's go have a hot fudge sundae. All this excitement of almost, but not quite, catching the plaid-pants crook has given me an appetite."

"Whatever you say. A hot fudge sundae sounds perfect." Just as perfect, she thought, as this entire day.

Five

Colonel Blackstone sat in his favorite leather chair and watched John-Trevor pace back and forth in front of the fire. He listened attentively as the younger man talked, not interrupting to ask questions, or to press for more details.

John-Trevor finally halted his trek and looked at the colonel. "So, there you have it." Sort of, he amended silently. He hadn't told the colonel about the kisses he'd shared with Paisley, about the new and unwelcome emotions that churned within him, about his burning desire to make love with Paisley Kane. "She is a very unique, very special young woman."

"As was her mother," the colonel said quietly. "Yes, I do hear so much of Kandi in what you're telling me about Paisley.

Granted, Kandi was more worldly, ran fast and far from commitment to one man, never wanting to relinquish independence."

"Paisley is the opposite on that subject," John-Trevor said. "She wants to marry and have children."

"So you said. But the basics are the same. Kandi's door was always open to anyone who needed a meal, a place to sleep, or just a shoulder to cry on. I resented that at times, because I wanted her all to myself whenever I could be with her. But Kandi was Kandi, and I learned to accept her as she was, as well as love her very deeply." He sighed. "If only I hadn't ruined it."

"Colonel, as you can gather from what I've told you, it's impossible to get Paisley to think about what her life would be like if she had money at her disposal. She's obviously wary of even fantasizing about a life in which she'd have everything she ever wanted or needed."

"Yes, our sins come back to haunt us, John-Trevor. Kandi may have forgiven me in time for my tactless approach in attempting to convince her to marry me, but she'd obviously been deeply wounded. She may not have been aware that she was teaching Paisley to have such a narrow view of life and money. It's my fault, all of it. But that was then, and this is now. What am I to do about Paisley?"

John-Trevor ran one hand over the back of

his neck. "I don't know. My assignment was just to gather facts, remember?"

"Well, forget that. I'm asking for your opinion."

"Colonel, I honestly don't know what to say. She's happy with her life and has gathered people around her to create the family she never had. She has a lot of friends, a wide variety of interests. I had to get her home early today because she was meeting with a group for dinner who are trying to save some bird or squirrel or . . . I do think she would like a chance to see Paris again, but she isn't making a big deal out of it. She just says she's happy the way she is."

"So, she hasn't revealed any longings, any dreams, except, perhaps, to visit Paris. And of course, to marry and have a baby."

"A bushel of babies."

Colonel Blackstone laughed softly. "Delightful. She does sound absolutely delightful, my daughter."

John-Trevor turned to look at the fire, his hands shoved into the back pockets of his jeans.

"She is," he said somberly. "I've never met anyone like her before, Colonel. She's fresh air and sunshine and innocence. She's come this far in life without being hurt, but if it were known she's your daughter, worth millions, she'd be a sitting duck for every con artist in the country. She'd be completely vulnerable."

"Not if she were involved with the right man," Colonel Blackstone said. "She'd be fine if there were someone to stand by her side and watch over her, not allow any rogues to take advantage of her soft and giving heart."

Pulling his hands free of his pockets, John-Trevor turned to frown at the colonel.

"Where are you going to get this guy? Order him from a Sears catalog? Come on, Colonel. Even if you released a statement to the press saying that Paisley wouldn't have access to your money until you died, the vultures would still be lurking in the shadows to take her for all they could get."

"Are you saying that I shouldn't tell Paisley I'm her father? That I should keep my will as it now stands with almost everything going to charities? Dammit, John-Trevor, she's my daughter, my flesh and blood, the only thing of real significance that I'm leaving behind on this earth."

"*I'm* not telling you what to do," John-Trevor said. "Hell, I wouldn't want the decision on my conscience. All I know is, I don't want to see Paisley hurt. She's so special, so . . . You should see her eyes. They're big and dark, and so damnably trusting. She's— Why are you smiling?"

"Smiling?" the colonel said, raising his eyebrows. "Am I? I'm an old man, John-Trevor. I can't be held accountable for everything I do."

"Oh, yeah? You may be a tad eccentric,

Colonel, but mentally you're sharp as a tack.
Don't pull this 'I'm an old man' junk on me.
It doesn't wash. Could we stick to the subject
at hand? Exactly what are you going to do
about Paisley?"

Colonel Blackstone laced his fingers across
his chest and smiled at the licking flames of
the fire.

"I don't know yet. However, I think I should
see her for myself. I'll decide at the time if I
should speak to her, but I definitely want to
see her, if only from a distance."

John-Trevor nodded. "That's understandable."

"You can't imagine the memories that
swept over me when you said that Paisley has
the stained-glass panel I gave Kandi. How
Kandi loved her rainbow of dreams."

"Rest gently on dreams," John-Trevor said
softly.

"I can hear Kandi saying those words." The
colonel sighed. "So many memories of so
many years ago. I want to see my daughter."

"I'll work something out and contact you."

"Fine, good. You're spending the night up
here, aren't you?"

"If you don't mind."

"I welcome your company." He stared up at
the ceiling. "Perhaps I should look over some
of the younger executives who work in my
various corporations. There might be a viable
candidate among them for a husband for
Paisley."

"No," John-Trevor said sharply. When the colonel looked at him in surprise, he cleared his throat. "What I mean is, Paisley believes in fate, just like Kandi did. If you decide to tell her of your existence, and it comes to light later that you played matchmaker, she's liable to be very angry."

"Then you don't think I should steer men in her direction?"

"No, definitely not. Don't do that."

Colonel Blackstone faked a yawn to disguise his smile. "All right, John-Trevor, no young men will be brought on the scene at this point. Well, I'm off to bed. Stay up as long as you like, and help yourself to the brandy. You've done an excellent job so far. I believe this will all be resolved quite soon."

"I'm glad *you* think so. In my opinion, it's a royal mess."

Colonel Blackstone pushed himself to his feet. "Things aren't always as they seem, John-Trevor. What appears to be terribly confusing is often simply solved. Good night."

"Good night, sir."

"Rest gently on your dreams, John-Trevor," the colonel added as he left the room.

"Rest gently . . . I don't have any dreams," John-Trevor said to the empty room. Or did he? "Hell," he muttered, and reached for the decanter of expensive brandy.

* * *

Early the next afternoon, John-Trevor stood outside a glass-enclosed cubicle and watched Paisley, who was sitting at a table in the small room.

She was wearing a headset with a pencil-thin microphone attached to it. A book was propped on a wooden stand on the table, and while John-Trevor couldn't hear her through the glass, he saw her lips move. She was reading the text aloud. Judging by her facial expressions, she was deeply engrossed in the story, and at one point she covered her heart with both hands in a dramatic gesture.

John-Trevor realized he was grinning like an idiot, and he didn't care who saw him. Paisley was wearing a black skirt and a bolero jacket over a bright red blouse, and she looked beautiful. And he was so damn glad to see her.

At breakfast that morning, he'd pressed Colonel Blackstone into admitting that he did, indeed, have more information on Paisley than he'd originally told John-Trevor. The colonel knew where she worked, that she drove a two-year-old compact car, that her checking account had a tendency to drop below the minimum balance, and that three people lived with her. Now, the colonel said, the next step was for him to see his daughter.

John-Trevor was snapped from his reverie

by a sudden motion behind the glass. Paisley had removed the headset and gotten to her feet. He rapped on the panel of glass, and she turned. A smile instantly lit up her face, and her dark eyes sparkled. She raised a finger and mouthed, "One minute," then returned her attention to the reel-to-reel tape machine sitting on the table. She pressed a button and mindlessly watched the tape rewind, her heart beating wildly.

John-Trevor had come for her! she thought. She'd missed him from the moment he'd walked out of her house the previous afternoon. Through the hours since, and on into her dreams as she slept, he had filled her mind . . . and her heart. And now he was there, smiling at her beyond the glass.

The machine clicked, startling her back to reality, and as she removed the rewound tape, her smile slowly faded.

At the moment, she and John-Trevor were separated by a wall of glass. All she had to do to be with him was open the door and join him.

But what about reality? she pondered. Were she and John-Trevor Payton from such different worlds that there was no hope of something special, wonderful, and forever growing between them?

She didn't know, but this, she told herself, was not the time to dwell on it. He was there, and she was so very glad to see him.

She crossed the room, opened the door,

and stepped out into the hall. As her gaze met John-Trevor's, any greeting she might have uttered was forgotten. She couldn't speak, could hardly breathe, as she drank in the sight of him.

Before he realized he'd moved, he had closed the distance between them. Framing her face in his hands, he stared down at her, feeling as though he were drowning in the dark pools of her eyes.

Then he lowered his head and kissed her.

There was no hesitancy, no tenderness. The kiss was instantly hot and urgent. Desperate for more contact with her, for anything that might ease the ache inside him, he dropped his hands and slid his arms around her. As he pulled her body against his, she sighed, and that soft sound inflamed even more than the sensation of her tongue's stroking his.

Paisley, Paisley. She was his. All his.

She gripped his arms as her legs began to tremble. His passionate kiss and embrace had swept away all of her good sense, tossing her into a whirlpool of desire. If he didn't stop soon, she thought hazily, she would not hold herself responsible for her actions.

As though he understood how close she was to giving in completely to him, John-Trevor lifted his head. He couldn't resist brushing his lips over hers once more, then he finally stepped back, dropping his arms from around her.

"Lord, what you do to me," he said, his voice husky. "I start kissing you and I don't seem to be able to stop. I want to make love to you, too, but you know that." He glanced around. "Well, you're safe here at least. I haven't ravished anyone in a library in a year or so." He dragged one restless hand through his hair. "Ignore me, Paisley. I'm just babbling while I try to get myself under control. You do manage to turn me inside out, lady."

"You—you do the same to me, John-Trevor," she said softly. "I missed you so much after you left yesterday. Maybe I should act coy and not tell you that, but it's the truth. I missed you, I'm so very glad to see you, and it seemed liked an eternity since you'd kissed me." She smiled. "Oh, and hello."

There was no matching smile on his face. "Hello," he said softly.

"You look like a brewing storm," she said, her smile fading, "What's wrong?"

"Nothing. Listen, I came by to see if you'd like to go out to dinner tonight."

Her bright smile instantly reappeared. "I'd love to."

"Good. Seven o'clock?"

"That's fine."

"Well, I'll see you tonight." He didn't move. "At seven. For dinner." He raised one hand as though to touch her, then curled his fingers into a fist and dropped it to his side.

He stepped around her and started down the hallway. "Bye."

Paisley turned to watch him disappear. "Bye," she whispered.

John-Trevor, she mused, switched moods so quickly, it was difficult to keep up. One minute he'd been kissing her—had he ever kissed her—and the next thing she knew, he seemed angry. Such a complicated man. Well, there was no sense in worrying about that now. She'd much rather concentrate on the fact that she was going out to dinner with him. She glanced at her watch and groaned. It was *hours* until seven o'clock.

John-Trevor sat behind the wheel of his rented car in the parking lot of the library, glowering out the windshield at a winter-bare tree. Why in the hell couldn't he figure out what the tangle of emotions he was feeling for Paisley meant? He *needed* to know before he totally lost his mind. Why couldn't he, detective extraordinaire, sort through and solve the twisted puzzle in his brain? Some detective he was.

He swore and shook his head.

He'd been kissing Paisley outside that little glass room practically before he'd realized he'd moved. One look at her and he'd been lost. If she appeared by his car at that very instant, he'd grab her, kidnap her back to his hotel, and not let her leave until the raging hunger in him had finally been slaked. What in the hell was she doing to him? What was happening to him? What—

Suddenly he stiffened and gripped the steering wheel so tightly, his knuckles turned white.

Oh, no, he thought fiercely. He would not, he *refused* to fall in love with Paisley Kane. Dammit, if that little whisper of a woman was making him fall in love with her, he'd wring her neck. He would not now or ever hand his heart to a woman on a silver platter to do with as she saw fit.

Paisley had better stop pushing his buttons. She had to quit looking at him the way she did with those gorgeous eyes of hers. And she could just knock off kissing him as if there were no tomorrow, and stop feeling like heaven itself when she nestled close to his hard, aching body.

Lord, how he wanted her. Wanted to make love with her, wanted to protect her from harm, wanted to be the only man who ever touched her.

Because . . .

"Dammit," he muttered, thunking his forehead against the steering wheel. "Payton, I'm going to shoot you with your own gun."

Because he was in love with Paisley Kane.

John-Trevor raised his head, narrowed his eyes, and twisted the key in the ignition. He roared out of the parking lot, refusing to think about anything. He simply blanked his mind and drove.

Hours later, John-Trevor listened absently as Paisley answered his question about what book she had been translating in the library that day. She chattered on as he divided his attention between the driving and her.

She looked sensational. She had a unique flair with clothes that probably stemmed from growing up in Paris. To wear three brightly colored silk men's ties, neatly knotted but with the knots pulled down several inches below the collar of her silky, creamy blouse, sounded weird, but it was striking.

With the blouse she wore a slim-fitting black wool skirt that flattered her small waist and nicely rounded hips. And her high-heeled black leather boots nearly made him salivate. Oh, yes, she was really sensational. He should have given more thought to his apparel, he decided. A dark suit, white shirt, and striped burgundy tie didn't have much pizzazz compared to Paisley's outfit.

And all this attention to clothes, John-Trevor silently admitted, was to take his mind off this dinner with Paisley. Colonel Blackstone would be somewhere in the restaurant so he could see his daughter for the first time.

John-Trevor had carefully picked the restaurant. He'd wanted semicasual but quiet, and a seating arrangement that was cozy, but not so intimate that others couldn't observe them . . . and be observed. He'd entered and rejected four establishments that afternoon before deciding he'd found the right one.

Inside the restaurant, the hostess showed them to a small table with a candle in a hurricane lamp in the center. Dim lights glowed in the ceiling, providing enough light to see the faces of the other diners. John-Trevor's quick scrutiny of the room did not reveal Colonel Blackstone.

He and Paisley ordered the prime rib, and a bottle of red wine. After the waitress had left the table, John-Trevor looked directly at Paisley, then immediately wished he hadn't. The candlelight poured over her, accentuating her fair skin, dark eyes, and the silken texture of the black curls that framed her face.

Lord, she was lovely, he thought, and delicate, like a china doll. His heart was going crazy again, pounding like a bongo drum, and a hungry heat was surging low in his body. He wanted her, and he was in love with her, and he'd never been in such a mess in his entire life.

"Do you have a boat?" she asked abruptly.

"What? A boat? No. Why?"

"Because you live in California."

"I have friends with boats. I'm not much

on sailing, though. It's too slow. I do like to water-ski."

"What else do you do for entertainment?"

He shrugged. "Go to movies, concerts. I read a lot, enjoy strolling through museums, and I attend any and all sports events that I can." He shifted slightly in his chair and swept his gaze over the room. No Colonel Blackstone. "I really enjoyed going to that museum with you yesterday. You're right, there's a lot to explore here. You'll have to give me another guided tour."

What was he saying? he asked himself. He had no business making future plans with her. But it sounded so right, and the words had come as naturally as breathing. "But," he said hurriedly, trying to backtrack, "you probably wouldn't want to if you've already been to most of the places."

"I'd enjoy every minute of showing Denver to you, John-Trevor," she said softly. "I'll be seeing it fresh through your eyes." Fate had to have a nudge at times, she reminded herself. "We'll definitely go on a grand tour . . . together, just the two of us."

"Perfect," he murmured, gazing into her eyes.

"Excuse me," a man said. Both Paisley and John-Trevor jumped in surprise, then looked up at the elderly man standing beside their table. "Your waitress was called away," he said, "so I'll be serving your dinner. Madam, if you will allow me . . ."

"Oh, yes, of course," Paisley said, moving her arms off the table so he could set her plate in front of her. "My that looks delicious."

The man turned to John-Trevor, "Sir?"

John-Trevor simply stared at the waiter—otherwise known as Col. William Blackstone!

Six

Colonel Blackstone turned to retrieve a small silver dish and spoon from his serving tray, set on a stand.

"Horseradish?" he asked Paisley.

"No, thank you."

The colonel looked at John-Trevor. "Sir?"

John-Trevor narrowed his eyes. "You're dishing out a lot more than just horse . . . radish."

"*Qu'avez-vous dit?*" the colonel asked, raising his eyebrows.

"Ah, you speak French," Paisley said, a smile lighting up her face. "How absolutely marvelous. *Avez-vous demeuré en France?*"

"Alas, no," the colonel said with a sigh. "I never actually lived in France. I visited Paris a great deal, though, many years ago."

"That's nice." John-Trevor said. "No, I

don't want any horseradish. Could we have our wine, please?"

"Of course," the colonel said. "I'll fetch it immediately."

"Isn't he sweet?" Paisley said as the colonel walked away.

"Cute as a button," John-Trevor said gruffly.

"You know, John-Trevor," she went on, frowning, "that waiter is rather elderly to be working at something this strenuous. That's terribly sad. He should be sitting at home, relaxing, enjoying his retirement. Don't you feel sorry for him?"

He'd like to murder Colonel Blackstone at the moment. But if he was fast enough on his feet, perhaps he could regain control of the situation.

"John-Trevor?" Paisley said. "Hello? I asked you if you felt sorry for our waiter because he has to work so hard at his age."

"Yes," John-Trevor said. "It's rough. How old do you think he is?" He paused. "About the age your father would be by now?"

"My father? How did he manage to get into this conversation?"

John-Trevor shrugged. "Frame of reference, that's all."

"Oh. Well, according to what my mother told me, my father would be in his early or midseventies by now. Yes. Just about the age of our waiter. I think it's wonderful when older people keep active, but being a waiter is very hard, physical labor. That dear man. My heart goes out to him."

"Mmm," John-Trevor said, then cut off a piece of his meat. "Eat."

"Yes, yes of course," Paisley said.

The colonel returned to the table, proceeded with the wine-tasting ritual with John-Trevor, then peered at Paisley's plate.

"You haven't had a bite," he said. "It's going to get stone cold. And don't ignore your broccoli. It's good for you. You can't just eat the flower, you know. You have to eat the stem as well."

"What?" Paisley asked, staring at him.

"Thank you, Mother Hubbard," John-Trevor muttered under his breath.

"Will there be anything else at the moment?" Colonel Blackstone asked.

"No!" John-Trevor said.

"Wait a minute," Paisley said. "What you just said about the broccoli, about having to eat the stem as well as the flower. Why did you say that?"

John-Trevor glanced at Paisley, then frowned in concern. "What's wrong, Paisley? You're very pale all of a sudden."

She didn't seem to hear him. Her attention was fixed on the waiter. "Why did you say that?" she repeated.

"Because there are a lot of vitamins in the stem," he answered. "It's very healthy, and you should eat the whole thing."

"My—my mother used to say that," Paisley

said, her voice not quite steady. "Almost exactly the same way. 'Paisley, you must eat the stem of your broccoli as well as the pretty flower.' And then she'd go on about the vitamins. How strange that you picked those very words."

Dammit, John-Trevor thought. The colonel was blowing it, speaking without thinking.

"Paisley," John-Trevor said, "a lot of mothers say stuff like that. James-Steven hated the crust on his toast, but our mom said he had to eat the frame as well as the buttery picture, or some such thing. It's Mother Jargon, it's in their job description." He looked at Colonel Blackstone. "Right?"

"What?" the colonel said. "Oh, yes. Of course. It's common to hear a mother refer to broccoli in terms of a flower and stem, or leaves and a trunk, all kinds of imaginative comparisons to get their little ones to eat it down to the last bite."

"Well, yes, I suppose that's true," Paisley said slowly. "It just startled me to hear you say it exactly the way my mother did. That, combined with your speaking French, brought back a great many memories. I'm sorry I overreacted to something as silly as broccoli."

"You're forgiven," John-Trevor said. "Well, don't let us keep you from your other pressing duties," he added to the colonel.

"You're my only customers," Colonel Blackstone said. "I don't move as fast as I used to, I'm afraid."

"They only assign you one table?" Paisley said. "How can you possibly make a living if— Excuse me. It's none of my business. We don't need anything else. Why don't you go rest until we're ready for dessert?"

"You're a dear child," the colonel said. "I *am* a tad weary. I'll go put my feet up and my bottom down." He walked away.

"John-Trevor," Paisley whispered, her eyes wide again.

"What is it?"

She leaned toward him. "Did you hear what he said? That was another of my mother's phrases. She'd come home from singing in a club and say. 'Oh, I'm exhausted. It's time to put my feet up and my bottom down.' That waiter knew my mother, John-Trevor, I'm certain of it. He's quoting her verbatim."

"Paisley, you're reading too much into this. It's my fault you're doing it because I've been bringing up the subject of your father. We meet an older man who has visited Paris, speaks French, happens to use sayings similar to your mother's, and . . . well, your imagination is working overtime. Eat your dinner."

Paisley frowned, but dutifully ate some of her baked potato.

"What if," John-Trevor said after a minute, striving for a casual tone, "your old buddy fate is doing its thing. Wouldn't it be something if that waiter really was your father?"

Paisley stiffened. "My . . . That's absurd."

"Yeah, I suppose it is. Let's forget about that guy and enjoy our dinner. Darn, I forgot to call my office and check in with my secretary. I'll be right back." He stood up. "This won't take long."

"Does your secretary work this late?"

"Oh. Well, I'll phone her at home. She lives just outside L.A. with six cats and a pet frog. Great lady." He strode away.

"Pet frog?" Paisley mumbled, then shrugged. She plunked one elbow on the table and rested her chin on her hand.

Wouldn't it be something, her mind echoed, *if that waiter really was your father?*

No, it wasn't possible. Or was it? When dealing with fate, anything was possible. Hadn't fate caused her to dump John-Trevor into the snowdrift? Absolutely. But would it then have her meet her father just a few days later? What a mind-boggling thought.

A ten-dollar bill pressed into the hand of the hostess gained John-Trevor the information he needed. He entered a small office off the lobby and found Colonel Blackstone sitting on a sofa. John-Trevor closed the door and glowered at the older man.

"What in the hell do you think you're doing?" he asked in a loud voice.

The colonel didn't seem at all perturbed at the younger man's tone. He simply smiled.

"You can't imagine, John-Trevor, what it was like to see Paisley for the first time. She's the very image of Kandi, so very beautiful. I had to get closer, can't you understand that? I had to speak to my daughter, hear her voice, see her smile."

"Yeah, okay. I get the drift. But you're blowing it, Colonel."

"I'm sorry about saying those things the way Kandi had said them. I didn't realize that's where I'd originally heard them."

"That's not the point, Colonel. You've met Paisley now, and it's based on lies. She thinks you're a poor old man who's forced to work terribly hard. What do you think is going to happen when she finds out the truth? She's so honest and trusting, and I'm building a tower of lies, and now so are you. We're dead meat. Lord, the thought of seeing the hurt in her eyes when she finds out . . ."

"You're in love with her."

"I didn't say that."

"You didn't have to. I knew when you were at my house yesterday. It's my fault you're having to lie to her." He shook his head. "I'm making a terrible mess of this."

"Look, Colonel, we've got to slow down, think this through. Have you definitely decided to tell Paisley you're her father?"

"No. There's so much money, John-Trevor, so much. What if it causes her nothing but grief, forces her to live a life that is wrong for her and brings her only unhappiness? I need time, and the opportunity to observe her for myself. I have to get into her house for a bit, watch her, listen to her. Will you help me, John-Trevor?"

"Colonel, we're talking *more* lies."

"There's no other choice at present. If she comes to love you as you love her, she'll forgive you for—"

"Whoa," John-Trevor interrupted, raising one hand. "I never said that I was going to tell Paisley that I love her. I'm not thrilled that I do, Colonel, because it's not the way I've set up my life. Lord, she even wants a bushel of babies." He stared up at the ceiling. "I can't handle this."

Colonel Blackstone stroked his chin, then got to his feet. "Any idiot can see you're the wrong man for my daughter."

John-Trevor's gaze collided with Colonel Blackstone's. "That's a helluva thing to say. I'm a decent, tax-paying citizen. I'm as good as any of those yuppie types you were going to parade under Paisley's nose."

"But you don't want to marry her. No, I'm sorry, John-Trevor, but you won't do."

"Now wait one damn minute here."

"John-Trevor, you'd better get back to your table before Paisley wonders where you are. I'll be out in a bit to see if you're ready for your dessert and coffee." He laughed. "I'll have you know I paid two hundred dollars for the dubious honor of filling your coffee cup. There's no time now to go into details about how I'm to get into Paisley's home. Just follow my lead when I make my move."

"Hell," John-Trevor muttered, then spun on his heel and left the room, slamming the door behind him.

Colonel Blackstone smiled. "Mr. and Mrs. John-Trevor Payton. Paisley Kane Payton. Ah, yes, it's perfect."

Paisley glanced idly around the restaurant, her gaze lingering on the other couples dining there. Then she stared at the empty chair across from her, and a sudden chill swept through her.

Even though John-Trevor had only gone to make a phone call, she felt dreadfully alone and for the first time in her life, lonely. It took little imagination to consider how she'd feel when he left permanently. The ache of tears tightened her throat, and her heart seemed clutched by an icy fist.

Since the moment she'd met John-Trevor Payton, her life had irrevocably been changed. She'd emerged from her safe cocoon of innocence and was now a woman ready for a loving, lasting commitment to a man. But what if that man wasn't ready, was never ready?

She looked up just as John-Trevor reentered the dining room and felt the instant quickening of her heart. Her blood seemed to hum in her veins, calling his name, urging him to move faster, to close the distance between them and replace the chill of loneliness with the welcome heat of passion.

He was so tall, she mused, and strong. And complicated, moody, stubborn, and infinitely gentle and caring.

He was John-Trevor Payton.

And she loved him.

He slid onto his chair and smiled at her. "Done. All is well at the office, everything under control." He took a bite of his meat. "A bit cold, but it's still good. You're about finished, I see, but I'll catch up, then we'll order dessert. Do you know what you'd like?"

"Pecan pie," she said, then a funny little giggle escaped from her lips.

The first words she said after discovering she was in love with John-Trevor were "pecan pie"? Not "I love you, John-Trevor." Not "Take me, I'm yours," but "pecan pie." That was something to tell the grandchildren—assuming she ever had any.

"Paisley," John-Trevor said, bringing her from her thoughts, "did I miss something? You have a sort of dreamy smile on your face. You must be really crazy about pecan pie."

"I love you, John-Trevor."

He choked on a sip of wine and barely

managed to set the glass down without spilling any.

"You what?" he asked, his voice croaking like the pet frog his secretary didn't have.

"I'm in love with you," she said pleasantly. "I thought I was, but I didn't know for certain until now. I love you, and there's no point in not telling you because you're the person I'm in love with, and you have the right to know."

"Paisley, you can't . . ." He glanced around. "You can't sit in a crowded restaurant and drop a bomb like that on a man."

"Why not? It's true. I do love you. Fate brought us together, John-Trevor. Of course, fate may have been a bit hasty since you're still set against marriage. But that doesn't change the fact that I truly love you with all my heart. And I want to *make* love with you too." She paused. "May I have my pecan pie now, please?"

"No!"

Heads turned in his direction, and he smiled weakly before closing his eyes for a moment. He took a steadying breath, then looked at Paisley again. He opened his mouth to speak, then snapped it closed.

She loved him. Paisley Kane was in love with him. That lovely, delicate, innocent woman sitting across from him had chosen him over the multitude of men in the world.

And he loved her. Lord, how he loved her.

He was throwing in the towel, giving up the fight to protect his heart at all costs.

He had lost, but he had won. He had won Paisley.

Warmth spread through him like rich brandy, filling him, stroking him with a comforting touch like nothing he'd known before. It encompassed his mind, his heart, his very soul, the essence of who he was.

He was in love, and he was loved by the most incredibly beautiful and enchanting woman he'd ever met.

Yes, he loved Paisley, but he'd be damned if he'd tell her that in the middle of a restaurant.

"John-Trevor," she said, "you have a very strange expression on your face. What are you thinking?"

"Pecan pie," he said quickly. "We'll have dessert now, okay?" He glanced around, and a moment later Colonel Blackstone appeared at the table. "We'll have pecan pie for dessert. I assume you have pecan pie?"

"I'll check," the colonel said. "If we do, shall I bring it with whipped cream?"

"Yes," John-Trevor said. "Paisley?"

"What? Oh, yes, whipped cream is nice."

"I shall return," Colonel Blackstone said.

"Paisley," John-Trevor said quietly as the colonel left, "I'm not ignoring what you said about . . . well, you know. I'd just rather not discuss it here. We'll have dessert, then go back to your house. If your crew is milling around, we'll go somewhere else."

"All right," Paisley said, meeting his gaze. "You're awfully serious, John-Trevor. Is this conversation we're planning to have going to make me cry? I'm a very noisy crier." She sighed. "I guess I shouldn't have told you that I love you right now. But I just suddenly knew, you see, and I thought you should know and . . . Oh, dear."

"Hey, don't upset yourself. We're going to have a long talk, remember? Here comes our dessert. Concentrate on that for now."

"Here we are, ma'am," Colonel Blackstone said, setting a plate with a huge piece of pie, whipped cream smothering it, in front of Paisley. "And for you . . . sir," he added, plunking another plate in the vicinity of John-Trevor's elbow. John-Trevor couldn't help noticing his piece was quite a bit smaller than Paisley's. "Is everything all right?"

"Dandy," John-Trevor said.

"You're sure?" the colonel asked, giving John-Trevor a hard, long look.

"May I have some coffee, please?" Paisley said.

"Of course," the colonel said. "And you, sir? Coffee? Or are you the *wrong* type of man to *join* the lady in her *desire* for . . . coffee?"

Cute, John-Trevor thought. Very cute. The colonel was making it clear he considered

John-Trevor to be the wrong man for Paisley. Well, tough.

"I definitely want exactly what the lady does," he said, scowling at the colonel.

"Mmm," Colonel Blackstone said, then stalked off.

Paisley took a bite of her pie and instantly realized she no longer wanted it. There was a lump in her throat and a knot in her stomach that made eating nearly impossible.

What was John-Trevor going to say? she wondered. Was he going to break it to her gently that he was flattered as all get out that she loved him, but sorry, babe, he just didn't love her? And then would he leave, taking her heart with him?

Would the diamond of stained glass she'd allotted him never glow with the promise of his love for her?

Was she destined to cry and cry and cry during the empty days and lonely nights ahead?

"Oh, *non*," she whispered.

"What's the matter?" John-Trevor asked. "Don't you like your pie? I think it's delicious, but you've probably been spoiled by Gracie's creations."

"It's fine pie," she said, forcing a smile. "Practically perfect pecan pie."

He chuckled. "Try saying that three times in a row."

She took another bite of the unwanted dessert.

John-Trevor frowned, noting Paisley's unhappy expression. What was wrong with her? He felt great, euphoric even, eager for the moment when he could be alone with her and tell her of his love.

Of course, his practical side reminded him, he had a lot more than that to tell her. Namely, the truth about why he was in Denver. But he couldn't tell her that if the colonel decided not to reveal himself to her. And if the colonel *did* tell her who he was, what effect would that have on Paisley, her life, her feelings for him? Would she set him aside as she explored the brave new world her father could offer her?

Well, damn, John-Trevor thought, he was thoroughly depressing himself. He'd come down from his emotional high with a jarring thud, and the practically perfect pecan pie now tasted like sawdust.

"Are you ready to leave?" he asked.

"Well, yes, whenever you're finished with your dessert. I can't eat mine. I'm much too full from dinner. And I really don't want any coffee."

"Me neither," he said, then looked around for the colonel so he could signal for the bill.

The hostess approached the table instead. "Your . . . waiter went off duty, sir. Here's your check. You may pay it at the cashier's counter in the lobby."

"Thanks." John-Trevor got to his feet, then assisted Paisley with her chair. So, the colonel had called it quits for the night, he mused. In that case, he'd leave a generous tip for whoever had to clear away their dishes. Had it been the colonel, he would have gotten zip.

A storm front had moved in while they'd been inside the cozy restaurant, and a whipping cold wind held the threat of snow. They hurried across the parking lot, then John-Trevor stopped dead in his tracks.

"What's wrong?" Paisley asked. "Come on, it's freezing out here."

John-Trevor strode forward, his jaw set in a hard line as he passed his car and continued down the row to an old, rusty vehicle with the hood up.

"Trouble?" he asked gruffly.

Colonel Blackstone straightened and smiled. "It's dead as a doornail."

"Where did you get this heap?" John-Trevor asked in a harsh whisper. "And what in the hell are you up to now?"

Paisley joined the pair. "Gracious, won't your car start?"

Colonel Blackstone sighed. "Alas, no, the poor ancient thing. Well, I'll go call a friend to come fetch me. It shouldn't take him more than an hour or so to get here. I do hope he hasn't been sipping the cooking sherry tonight. At his age he can't see all that well as it is, let alone when he's tipsy."

Paisley shook her head. "I don't think you should call him if there's a chance he's . . .

No, that will never do. Don't you have any other friends?"

"None with cars."

"Well, that settles it then. You come home with me and phone from there. If your friend is indisposed, John-Trevor and I will take you home. You simply can't stay out in this weather."

"Paisley," John-Trevor said, "you can't take home men you don't know."

"I took *you* home, John-Trevor."

"That was different," he said, his volume rising.

"Why?" Paisley and the colonel asked in unison.

"Because—because . . ." He threw up his hands.

"So much for that argument," Paisley said cheerfully. "Shall we go before we all freeze?"

"Splendid," the colonel said. "Thank you from the bottom of my heart, my dear. Oh, my name is Blackstone. William Blackstone."

"I'm Paisley Kane, and this glowering man is John-Trevor Payton."

"A pleasure, sir," the colonel said.

"Yeah, right," John-Trevor muttered, then spun on his heel and strode to his car.

During the drive to Paisley's, John-Trevor found, to his own amazement, that he was actually relaxing and enjoying the ongoing chatter between Paisley and the colonel. He'd never seen the colonel so animated and full of life, and constantly smiling.

Paisley was being her usual open self, and the pair had really hit it off. It was nice, terrific, in fact, to witness this meeting of father and daughter, even though Paisley didn't know she was the daughter.

As he stopped in front of Paisley's house, she broke off what she was saying to the colonel and gasped.

"Something is wrong," she said. "Look at how many lights are on. The place is lit up like a Christmas tree. Hurry, William, open the car door. I have to get inside."

Colonel Blackstone got out of the car, then Paisley ran to the house with John-Trevor and the colonel close behind her. She dashed inside without touching the stained-glass panel. Colonel Blackstone stared at the panel for a moment, then hurried in, John-Trevor at his heels.

Bobby came racing out of the kitchen. "Paisley! Oh, man, I'm glad you're here."

"Bobby, what is it?"

"It's Maxine. She's in labor . . . the puppies . . ." His voice caught. "Dammit, Paisley, something is wrong. Something terrible is wrong with Maxine."

Seven

Coats were hung haphazardly on the brass tree, then Paisley, John-Trevor, and Colonel Blackstone followed Bobby into the kitchen.

The professor, wearing a bulky, faded gray sweater, and baggy black slacks, stood at the far side of the room, wringing his hands. Gracie, again wearing her head-to-toe bright blue ensemble, was making a pot of tea.

"Maxine's in the laundry room," Bobby said. "I made her a nice bed with newspapers on the bottom and old towels on top. But, dammit, Paisley, I don't know what else to do."

"Take it easy, son," Colonel Blackstone said, placing one hand on Bobby's shoulder. "By the way, I'm William Blackstone. Let's have a look at the patient, shall we?"

"Oh, I'm sorry," Paisley said. "I didn't make

introductions." She quickly rattled off the necessary names.

"Come on," Bobby said, shifting from one foot to the other. "Maxine is all alone in there. Come on!"

John-Trevor walked behind Paisley, but at the door of the laundry room he saw there wasn't space enough for all of them. As the colonel hunkered down with Bobby in front of Maxine, John-Trevor placed his hands on Paisley's shoulders, stopping her just outside the door.

"We'll only be in the way," he said. "Let's wait here."

"All right," Paisley said, staring into the small room. "Maxine is breathing so hard. I thought puppies just . . . popped out."

"I think they're supposed to. I don't really know anything about this."

"I've made tea," Gracie said behind them. "Crises call for tea. Would anyone care for a cup?"

"No, thank you, Gracie," Paisley and John-Trevor said in unison.

"Bobby is so upset," Gracie went on. "I've never seen him like this. And our poor, darling Maxine. She's gotten so weak she can't even lift her head. Why don't those puppies get themselves born?"

"I'm sure she'll be all right," Paisley said. "She has to be."

John-Trevor tightened his hold on her shoulders. "Stay calm, okay? We're all here, and we'll get Maxine whatever help she needs."

"Thank you, John-Trevor," Paisley whispered.

Colonel Blackstone got to his feet, patted Bobby on the back, then returned to the kitchen.

"Telephone?" he asked.

"On the wall there," Paisley said. "William, do you know what's wrong with Maxine?"

"Not beyond the fact that she doesn't seem able to deliver those puppies." He picked up the receiver and punched in some numbers. "Suite nine oh seven, please," he said, then, "George? Do you have a pencil and paper? Good. I'd like you to go to the address I'm going to give you and pick up Dr. Samuel Morley. Just tell him I sent you and that it's an emergency. Then bring him here, to this other address I'm about to give. Ready?"

As the colonel dictated the two addresses, Paisley looked up at John-Trevor in confusion. "This doesn't make sense," she said. "Who's George? I thought the only friend he had who owned a car lived an hour away and sipped cooking sherry."

The colonel hung up and started back toward the laundry room.

"William," Paisley said, "who's George?"

"My chauffeur. He'll pick up a veterinarian friend of mine and bring him over here in my town car." He glanced at his watch. "He shouldn't be too long. The hotel we're staying at is only about five minutes from Sam's place, and it should take him another ten minutes to drive here."

Paisley shook her head. "Hotel? Chauffeur? Town car?"

"I'll stay in here with Bobby," the colonel added. "Show Sam in the moment he arrives, will you please?"

"Yes, of course, but—"

"My, he certainly is a distinguished-looking man, isn't he?" Gracie said as the colonel rejoined Bobby. "And he's so competent, has that take-charge type of personality. Where on earth did you find him, Paisley?"

"You wouldn't believe me if I told you, Gracie." She studied John-Trevor. "William is *not* who he presented himself to be."

"Yeah, well . . ." John-Trevor stared at a spot somewhere above her head. "That's . . . uh, not the issue right now. He's getting help for Maxine, and that's what's important. We'll worry about the other later."

"But—"

"Later, Paisley."

She sighed. "Okay. Everything will be fine, just fine. Maxine will come through this with flying colors and will be a wonderful mama to her babies."

"You bet," John-Trevor said.

"Have some tea," Gracie said. "I do wish Bobby would have a cup. He's so distraught. Maxine means the world to him."

"I don't think Bobby wants any tea at the

moment," John-Trevor said gently, "but you have it ready in case he changes his mind."

The professor just kept wringing his hands.

Silence fell, and the minutes slowly passed as John-Trevor and Paisley resumed their vigil at the doorway to the laundry room. John-Trevor returned his hands to her shoulders, and several times had to resist the urge to drop a kiss on the top of her head. He also resisted inching her backward to nestle against him. When she sighed, though, he did give her shoulders a gentle squeeze.

I love you, Paisley Kane, he told her silently. And all he could do at the moment was hope that their combined love was strong enough to weather the storm of his duplicity.

When the tinny tune of "Here Comes Peter Cottontail" reverberated through the air, he jerked in surprise, then dropped his hands from Paisley's shoulders, and she raced to answer the door.

Less than a minute later, she returned with a pleasant-appearing man in his fifties who carried a black medical bag, and another burly man in his sixties who wore a black suit and had a billed cap tucked under his arm.

Any second now, John-Trevor thought, he was going to hear . . .

"Good evening, Mr. Payton," George said. "I didn't know *you* were here."

"Yeah, well," John-Trevor said, throwing up his hands, "here I am, George."

Paisley shot John-Trevor a quick, confused glance, then turned to the man with the medical bag.

"We'll cover introductions later," she said. "Please, Doctor, go right in that room there and help Maxine."

"Don't worry about a thing," Dr. Morley said. He crossed the kitchen and entered the laundry room. "Hello, William. What seems to be the problem?"

"Would you care for a cup of tea?" Gracie asked George.

"Why thank you, ma'am," George said. "That would sure hit the spot right about now."

Gracie beamed. "Oh, good. Someone finally wants a cup of my tea."

A low murmur of voices could be heard from the laundry room as Gracie bustled back and forth, delivering tea and cinnamon-apple muffins to the table.

Paisley stared at John-Trevor, her eyes narrowed. "You and I," she said quietly, "need to have a little chat later, Mr. Payton."

He gave her his hundred-watt smile. "Really?"

She did not smile back. "Really."

His smile disappeared as quickly as it had come. "Oh."

Ten silent minutes passed with Paisley and John-Trevor staring at the laundry-room door, Gracie and George consuming tea and muffins, and the professor continuing to wring his hands.

Suddenly Dr. Morley appeared, carrying Maxine wrapped in a blanket.

"George," the veterinarian said, "let's go. Quickly now, there's no time to waste. I need to get Maxine to my office. William, you and Bobby can ride with me."

"We'll follow you," Paisley said, "but what exactly is wrong?"

"Maxine was apparently injured in the past," the doctor said, "and there's scar tissue blocking the birth canal. I'll have to operate immediately to have any hope of saving her and the puppies."

"Oh, *Mon Dieu*," Paisley exclaimed. "Go on. Hurry. We'll be right behind you."

"I'll stay here and keep the tea hot," Gracie said. "Be brave, Bobby. Maxine is in good hands."

Everyone grabbed his coat and tumbled out the front door. A few minutes later, John-Trevor was convinced that George had been a race car driver in a former life, and it took every bit of his concentration to keep the black town car in sight.

Paisley stared out the side window, one part of her mind centered on Maxine, while the other part desperately tried to make sense of the evening. Disjointed scenes and conversations with both John-Trevor and William Blackstone played over and over again. Mr. Blackstone, she now knew, was far from being an object of sympathy. He apparently had plenty of money. He had a chauffeur, for heaven's sake. He was playing some kind of strange game . . . and John-Trevor Payton was one of the players.

With increasing force, one message was emerging from the tangle in her mind. John-Trevor had lied to her.

The man she loved, the man she'd given her heart to, the man she had carefully placed in her stained-glass rainbow of dreams, had lied.

Dear Lord, that hurt.

John-Trevor had known William Blackstone before that evening. He had been greeted by name by the older man's chauffeur! He had entered her world not by fate, but by design.

She turned her head and looked at him. *Why, John-Trevor?* she silently asked him. *Why did you lie to me?* Even more, how *much* had he lied to her? Had their kisses meant nothing to him? Had his interest in her, the questions he'd asked her, the smoldering gazes he'd sent her way, all been part of the role he was playing?

She had to know the truth. She would *demand* to be told the truth. And when she heard it, whatever it was, she had the sad, sickening feeling it would shatter her heart.

John-Trevor screeched to a halt as the town car stopped in front of a small, one-story brick building. Moments later, he and Paisley were running after the others into the building.

Maxine in his arms, Dr. Morley disappeared through a swinging wooden door. The rest of them stood motionless, staring at the door as though expecting a neon sign to flash a report as to what was happening.

"Well," the colonel said, breaking the tense silence, "now we wait. I suggest we take off our coats and sit down."

"No," Bobby said. "I'm not moving. Maxine might need me. Maxine counts on me to be there whenever . . ." His voice was choked with emotion. "I sure as hell screwed this up. I knew something was wrong, but I didn't know what to do to help her." He shook his head. "Oh, God, Maxine, I'm sorry."

Paisley gripped Bobby's upper arms and looked him straight in the eye. "You mustn't blame yourself for this," she said firmly. "It's not your fault. You *were* there when Maxine needed you, and now she's getting the best care available. Please, come sit down."

"You don't understand, Paisley," he said, fighting against his tears. "Maxine is my dog. Mine. I've never had a dog. I've never had *anyone* who needed me like she does. I mean, yeah, we're a family, you, Gracie, the professor, but it wouldn't matter all that much if I weren't around. But with Maxine, it *did* make a difference that I was there. She trusted me, you know what I mean? Whatever I said or did, it was okay. She wagged her tail and smiled at me. She really smiled, Paisley, honest to God she did."

"I know," Paisley whispered as two tears slid down her cheeks. "I know, Bobby."

"Dammit," Bobby said, a sob catching in his throat, "I don't want her to die. I wouldn't know how to handle that. She's sort of ugly and stuff, but I think she's great, and I—I really . . . love her. I really love her, Paisley."

"Oh, Bobby," she said, flinging her arms around him.

John-Trevor swallowed heavily past the lump in his throat, then glanced up just as Colonel Blackstone looked at him. Tears shimmered in the old man's eyes. As though they'd spoken aloud, the two men exchanged messages.

I love your daughter, John-Trevor told the colonel.

I love my daughter, the colonel answered.

And, dammit, I don't want anything to happen to Maxine. Or to Bobby.

No, the colonel responded. *Neither do I.*

George pulled out a large white handkerchief, wiped his eyes, then blew his nose with a sound that could easily have been mistaken for a honking goose. John-Trevor and the colonel blinked, the eerie spell between them broken.

"Let's sit down, Bobby," Paisley said gently.

Slipping off her coat, she led him to the row of plastic chairs against the wall. Bobby sat down, propped his elbows on his knees, and buried his face in his hands. Paisley rested one hand on his back.

John-Trevor hesitated, then shrugged out of his jacket and sat next to Paisley. He took her free hand in his, and while she didn't attempt to pull away from him, neither did she acknowledge his presence.

Twilight Zone, John-Trevor thought. It was as though they were in limbo, like a freeze-frame in a movie. Paisley and John-Trevor were temporarily on hold while everything centered on Maxine. That was fine, he assured himself. He sure as hell wasn't in any rush to be confronted by Paisley with the evidence that he had lied to her.

If it hadn't been for the colonel and Maxine, he and Paisley would be alone now, declaring their love and making love. Oh, yes, making slow, sweet, sensual love through the entire night.

Vivid, tantalizing images shot through his mind, and he shifted in his chair as his body reacted to those images.

The real thing would be a heck of a lot better than images, he admitted ruefully. But the crazy thing was, even if threatened with bodily harm, he wouldn't budge from that chair until he knew that Maxine was going to be all right. If Paul-Anthony and James-Steven knew about this, they'd laugh themselves sick.

Bobby raised his head and took a deep

breath. "What's taking so long? That doctor said on the way over here that he'd have to operate, take the puppies by . . . whatever that fancy word was. But how come it's so slow? What's going on in there?"

" 'Patience.' " Colonel Blackstone said, " 'is the best remedy for—' "

" '—every trouble,' " Paisley finished. She slowly stood up, her hand slipping from John-Trevor's grasp as she stared at the colonel. "That was said by Titus Maccius Plautus. It was also said time and again, for a multitude of circumstances, by my mother. This is one coincidence too many, Mr. William Blackstone. There is no longer any doubt in my mind that you knew my mother."

Hell, John-Trevor thought.

The colonel stood and looked at her, an expression of obvious distress on his face. "Paisley, my dear," he said, "surely you realize that this is neither the time, nor the place, to discuss the subject of—"

Suddenly the wooden door swung open and Dr. Morley strode into the room. Bobby jumped up and met the veterinarian halfway across the room.

"Maxine?" Bobby asked anxiously. "How is she? Is Maxine okay?"

Dr. Morley smiled and placed one hand on Bobby's shoulder. "She's quite a girl, your Maxine. She's doing fine, son. She's a fighter, that one. I wouldn't have given you a plug nickel for her chances when I brought her in here, but she came through the surgery like a champ."

"Thanks." Bobby rubbed one sleeve quickly across his eyes. "I mean that, Doc. Thanks a lot."

"Oh," Paisley said, sniffling. "This is wonderful." She turned and flung herself against John-Trevor's body.

He automatically embraced her, holding her tightly. She sniffled some more and made funny little hiccuping sounds. He smiled down at the top of her head, absently deciding that he would not ever relinquish his hold on her.

"Anyone interested in babies?" Dr. Morley asked, laughing. "Two boys, two girls. Fat and sassy, and fit as fiddles."

"Oh-h-h," came Paisley's muffled response from the front of John-Trevor's chest.

Bobby blinked. "Wow. No kidding? Four? Man, that's awesome. Maxine had four puppies. Can I see her and the babies?"

"Just for a moment," Dr. Morley said. "She's still asleep from the anesthesia. The puppies are in a special incubator that has been equipped to allow them to nurse. Come have a look, Bobby, but it would be best if the rest of you remained here."

As Bobby disappeared through the door with Dr. Morley, Paisley slowly lifted her head to look at John-Trevor.

"Hi," he said, smiling down at her. "Feeling better?"

She sniffled. "Yes, I'm just so happy that Maxine is all right." She should move away from John-Trevor Payton that very instant, she told herself, put as much distance between them as possible. He'd lied to her. Lied! And she had to square off against William Blackstone, too, and demand to be told the truth about his knowing her mother. But it was so safe and warm in John-Trevor's embrace. He was so strong and smelled so good, and the heat emanating from him was now swirling deep within her. She loved him so very much. "Maxine had a bushel of babies."

John-Trevor chuckled. "She did, indeed." His smile faded. "I'm glad Maxine is going to be fine. She's an ugly mutt, but she grows on a guy. I'm going to bury the hatchet with Bobby too. After what I saw here tonight, I realize he's a caring, decent kid. That chip on his shoulder is just his way of protecting himself, I guess."

"Yes, that's exactly what it is. He'd do everything he could to help any of us in his family." She stiffened and moved back, forcing John-Trevor to drop his arms from around her. "Family. My mother. William Blackstone knew my mother, and you, Mr. Payton, know William Blackstone." She planted tight fists on her hips. "It's time for some answers."

"It's time for a soothing cup of tea," Colonel Blackstone interjected quickly. "It's been a stressful evening and our nerves are frazzled. Why don't we all go to Paisley's and calm down with a cup of tea made by that lovely Gracie?"

Before Paisley could answer, Bobby and Dr. Morley reemerged from the rear area.

"Good night, all," the doctor said. "Call me tomorrow, Bobby, and I'll let you know if Maxine can go home. From what I've seen of her so far, I'm betting she'll bounce right back from this and be ready to tend to her puppies."

"My thanks, Sam," Colonel Blackstone said. "You're the hero of the hour."

"You'll get my bill," Dr. Morley said, smiling.

"Yes, do send it directly to me," the colonel said.

"I wonder if Gracie has some more of those muffins," George said thoughtfully. "The lady surely makes fine muffins." He paused. "Why does she have bright blue hair?"

"She's color-blind," Bobby said. "You'd better tell her it looks great, or you'll answer to me."

"It *does* look great. She's a fine figure of a woman, that Gracie, and those muffins of hers are straight from heaven."

"You should taste her chocolate cake," Bobby said. "She puts whipped cream and—"

"*Aaak!*" Paisley screamed.

The occupants of the room were instantly quiet, and all eyes were riveted on her.

"That's better," she said, lifting her chin. "I am, of course, relieved and grateful that Maxine is out of danger. That crisis is over. However, there *is* a matter of importance that needs to be discussed."

"Paisley . . ." John-Trevor started.

"Quiet," she said, glaring at him.

He cleared his throat. "You bet."

"Thank you. Now then. John-Trevor, I assume that you still have the hotel room you stayed in last night?"

"Yes. I—"

"Fine. George, please take Bobby back to the house. Then, George, stay there and eat Gracie's muffins until such time as Mr. Blackstone calls to request that you pick him up. John-Trevor, Mr. Blackstone, and I will be going to John-Trevor's hotel room to have a conversation that is now overdue."

"Yes, ma'am," George said, then to his own amazement, he executed a crisp salute.

"Gentlemen," Paisley said, "shall we go?" She marched toward the door.

Paisley Kane was fantastic, John-Trevor thought. He was actually witnessing an exquisite example of the cliché "She's beautiful when she's angry." Absolutely sensational.

"Angry," however, he mused, did not quite cut it as far as describing Paisley's frame of mind. She was royally ticked off, and if he valued his life, he'd better follow orders and haul his butt out the door. Oh, Lord, how he loved that woman.

The drive to John-Trevor's hotel was made in total and extremely tense silence, as was the trip in the elevator up to the sixteenth floor.

Paisley stared straight ahead, her arms folded firmly beneath her breasts. John-Trevor and Colonel Blackstone exchanged a "We're in a heap of trouble, pal" glance, then the trio trudged down the carpeted hallway.

John-Trevor's room was, in actuality, a suite with a living room and a separate bedroom. Coats were removed, then with a rather defeated-sounding sigh, John-Trevor swept one arm in the direction of a grouping of easy chairs.

After they were seated, Paisley opened her mouth to speak, but Colonel Blackstone raised one hand.

"May I have the floor?" he asked.

She dipped her head in agreement, her expression stormy.

"Paisley," he said, his voice quiet and steady, "old men, such as myself, have a tendency to sit for hours looking back over their lives, reliving special events, cherishing memories. Of all the years I've been on this earth, I've come to realize that the happiest days—and nights—were those I spent with your mother."

"I knew it," Paisley said with a sharp nod of her head. Her expression didn't soften one iota. "There was no longer any doubt in my mind that you had known my mother. When did you—"

"Please," the colonel said, "let me have my say. Just hear me out, if you would be so kind, my dear."

"Proceed," she said stiffly.

John-Trevor propped his elbows on the arms of his chair and made a steeple of his fingers over the bridge of his nose.

"Kandi Kane," the colonel went on, "was the most beautiful, vivacious, incredibly unique woman I had ever met. For the first, and only, time in my life, I fell in love. I was very deeply in love with your mother. She cared for me, of that I'm certain, but more precious to her was her freedom and independence. She was an elusive butterfly who was not meant to be held in anyone's hand, but to flit through life, living each breathless moment to the fullest."

"A butterfly," Paisley whispered. "Yes. Yes, she would have liked that comparison."

"I loved her enough," Colonel Blackstone continued, "to walk out of her life when she asked me to. Her happiness was more important to me than my own, and so I left her. I did, however, hurt her in the process, and I'll never forgive myself for that. But the issue at hand is the present, and the fact that I've discovered that I did not, after all, leave Kandi all alone. I am, my darling child, your father."

Paisley pressed trembling fingers to her lips and closed her eyes for a moment, struggling to control her emotions.

John-Trevor watched her, his jaw clenched so tightly that his teeth ached. She looked fragile and vulnerable, he thought. He wanted to gather her into his arms, tell her that he loved her, and that whatever lay ahead, they would face it together.

She dropped her hand to her lap and opened her eyes. "You didn't know about me," she said, her voice unsteady. "I'm aware of that. My mother never told me who you were, but it was all right because she explained it to me so beautifully. She said you gave her two precious gifts, me and . . ."

"And the stained-glass panel," the colonel finished for her. "Kandi's rainbow of dreams."

"Yes." Tears slid down Paisley's cheeks, and John-Trevor nearly groaned aloud as he forced himself to stay in his chair.

Colonel Blackstone quietly explained why Kandi had purchased the house in Denver, how she'd left things in the hands of fate, yet had planned to tell Paisley on her twenty-first birthday who her father was. But since Kandi had died, the decision about revealing his identity had been up to him.

"And now you know," he said, "but I'm going one step farther."

"What do you mean?" she asked.

"I'm your father, Paisley, and it would be wonderful beyond words to be a part of your life for the remainder of my days. I'm a very wealthy man, *very* wealthy, and as my daughter you would inherit all that I have . . . except for sums I've set aside for a few people, like George, who have been important to me."

The colonel got to his feet. "But you see, the ball, as they say, is now in your court. The final decision is *yours* to make. Being publicly acknowledged as my daughter will thrust you into a world you may not enjoy. To suddenly have a father after never having one may not be what you want."

"But . . ." she began.

"Think it through carefully, Paisley," he said. "If you wish to step into the shoes of being Colonel William Blackstone's daughter, John-Trevor knows how to find me. If you decide not to, then be assured that I will respect your choice. I love you enough, as I did Kandi, to leave you in peace, if that will bring you the happiness you deserve." He swallowed heavily. "I'll—I'll call George from the lobby. Good night, my child. I'll be waiting to learn if this has been good-bye as well."

He turned and left the suite, closing the door behind him with a quiet click.

The sudden silence was oppressive. Paisley drew in a deep breath, then stared down at her hands.

"I'd—I'd like to go home now, John-Trevor," she said, hardly above a whisper.

John-Trevor narrowed his eyes and stared at her for a long moment before he spoke one word in a voice that did not invite debate.

"No."

Eight

Paisley's head snapped up, and she dashed the tears from her cheeks in a quick, jerky motion.

"No?" she repeated. She sat up straight as a pencil, her frown deepening to a definite glower. "Just what do you mean by 'No'?"

Slowly, John-Trevor stood and crossed the room to her. Gripping the arms of her chair, he leaned over until his face was nearly touching hers. She moved back as far as she could.

"It's the opposite of 'Yes,'" he said, his voice very low. "I am *not* taking you home now, Paisley. Not a chance."

"Well, why on earth not?" she said, hoping she sounded extremely indignant. John-Trevor was so close to her, so temptingly close. She wanted to sink her fingers into his thick hair, bring his lips to hers, and kiss him until they were both breathless. That would most definitely be giving fate a helpful nudge in the proper direction. But no, she had to remember that John-Trevor had lied to her, was a part of the almost unbelievable scenario involving William Blackstone . . . her father. Dear Lord, William Blackstone was her father! "Well?" she repeated. "Are you going to answer me?"

"I'm protecting my interests," he said. "You've just learned something that probably hasn't even begun to sink in. It's one thing to sit around playing 'what if' about your father. It's quite another to actually sit in the same room with a man who says, 'Paisley Kane, I am your father.' A man who happens to be worth millions of dollars."

"What does all that have to do with your holding me captive here?"

"It's very simple, Paisley. You're going to sift and sort through all this stuff that's been dumped on you, and somewhere in the middle of that mess you'll realize that I lied to you about why I was in Denver."

"I have, sir, already figured that out."

"And you're mad as hell."

"Well, yes, I'm very angry and"—she tried to hold her voice steady—"and hurt, too, because I thought that you and I . . . That is, I believed that something special was . . . And I made a fool of myself in that restaurant when I told you that I love you . . . But you were, I guess, checking me out, or whatever, for my—my father, and it was lies, all of it and . . . John-Trevor, I want to go home."

"No."

"Would you cut that out? You can't keep me here against my will. It's illegal. So quit saying no."

"No. No, I won't take you home now. And no, it was not all lies. And yes, there was, and is, something very special, and very important, happening between us. No, you did *not* make a fool of yourself at the restaurant by telling me that you love me because . . ." He shook his head. "Hell, I'm doing this all wrong. You've had so much thrown at you tonight, your brain circuits are probably going to blow a fuse."

He straightened and dragged one hand through his hair. "Paisley, listen, okay? I hated lying to you, I swear I did, but I was caught in the middle between you and Colonel Blackstone. I've known and worked for him for years, and I respect him very much. But believe me, I wasn't brought in here to determine if you passed some kind of test, if you were good enough to be acknowledged as the colonel's daughter. It wasn't anything like that at all. His main concern is what will truly bring you the most happiness."

John-Trevor began to pace back and forth in front of Paisley's chair. She watched him with wide eyes, her head swiveling back and forth as though she were observing a tennis match.

"What Colonel Blackstone said here tonight," he continued, "was the absolute truth. He'll respect your wishes, your choice, when you reach a decision regarding him. As for me, yes, I lied about what I was doing in Denver, and my references to your unknown father weren't idle chitchat. But—oh, hell, what can I say to convince you that every-thing else was real, that I fell in love with you, *am* in love with you? Lord knows, I didn't *want* to fall in love with you, but I sure as hell did. But why should you believe me, knowing that I lied to you?"

"I believe you, John-Trevor," Paisley said, fresh tears filling her eyes.

"The lies are there, dammit. They're like a wall between us, keeping us from—" He stopped dead in his tracks and stared at her. "What? What did you say?"

"I said, I believe you. The lies were a means to an end, so that you could carry out your assignment for Colonel Blackstone. I under-stand that now. I'm so happy because you love me, and I love you, and that proves that fate does need a nudge at times. I do love you so much, and I think it would be very appropriate if you kissed me right now. I— oh!"

She gasped as John-Trevor hauled her out of the chair and brought his mouth down hard onto hers. In the next instant, the kiss gentled, tongues met, and passions soared.

She raised her arms to encircle his neck as he nestled her close to his body, his arousal pressing against her. Their hearts raced and their breathing became labored as they took more, gave more, savored more, and wanted so much more.

John-Trevor loved her, Paisley thought, dazed. He was every color in her rainbow of dreams, the sunshine that would cause the stained glass to glow with vibrant beauty on the bleakest day. He was her life, the other half of who she was. He was John-Trevor, and she loved him.

Her breasts ached with a foreign sensitivity that she instinctively knew could be soothed by John-Trevor's touch. The pulsing heat deep within her was desire that only he could satisfy.

He would consume her, she mused hazily, fill her with all that he was. They would be one, from this day forward, a united force with a foundation of love, ready to face the unknowns of tomorrow.

He'd done it, John-Trevor thought as the blood thundered in his veins. For the first time in his life, he'd told a woman that he loved her. No, not "a woman," but Paisley. *His* Paisley. He loved her, and she loved him, and oh, Lord, it was fantastic.

He couldn't even remember why he'd vowed years ago never to love. It had to be fate. Fate had put his emotions on hold until he could find Paisley. And he was never going to let her go.

But . . .

He raised his head and took a ragged breath. "Paisley," he said, not releasing his hold on her.

"Hmmm?" she said dreamily, slowly opening her eyes.

"We have to cover a few things."

"Now?"

"Yes. Think about this, will you? I've known from the beginning that you're Colonel Blackstone's daughter, and you're in a position to be a very wealthy woman. How do you know I'm not just after your money?"

"Are you?"

"No, of course not."

She smiled. "Well, that takes care of that, doesn't it?"

He shook his head. "You're so trusting, so willing to accept people as they present themselves to you, never questioning their motives. Paisley, what are you going to do about Colonel Blackstone?"

Her smile faded. "Oh, John-Trevor, I don't want to think about that now. My mother always said I should have a good night's sleep before I make a major decision. I'm trying to grasp the fact that Colonel Blackstone is my father, but it just bounces around in my head with no place to land. I can't dwell on that now."

"But—"

"Please, John-Trevor, can't we concentrate on us tonight, on our love for each other? This is a glorious moment in our lives, and nothing else matters right now."

"It's not that simple, Paisley. Our love and the fact that Colonel Blackstone is your father are intertwined, because he's offering you more than you've ever dreamed of having."

"I realize that, but it wouldn't change how I feel about you."

"It might. I don't think you comprehend yet what is out there for you. Don't you see, Paisley? I couldn't handle it if our love kept you from having what I'd never be able to give you. Or what if you chose the colonel, and then discovered that you didn't like being in the public eye all the time, the way he has been for most of his life? And then you and he have years to catch up on. You'd be torn between wanting to spend time with him and time with me. This is an awful lot to deal with all at once."

Paisley studied him in silence for a moment, wondering why he suddenly seemed so anxious. And why did he talk about having to *choose* between him and her father? Why couldn't she have both? Then, with her newfound womanly wisdom, she understood. John-Trevor was scared of being in love. He'd been able to tell her of his feelings, but years of wariness would not be so easy to overcome.

Smiling seductively, she reached up to kiss him lightly. "I understand what you're saying, John-Trevor. Sort of. But tonight . . ." She kissed one corner of his mouth, then the other. "Tonight I intend to focus on us. Just us. I love you, John-Trevor, and I want to make love with you." She pressed her hips against his, thrilled when he groaned. "You *do* want to make love with me, don't you? Don't you, John-Trevor?"

"Oh, hell," he muttered, then his mouth captured hers.

Even as desire erupted within him, John-Trevor tried to pull back, telling himself that this wasn't the right time, that Paisley had enough to deal with. He had to stop. He had to—

"Love me, John-Trevor," she whispered against his lips. "I've waited so very long for you, for this moment, for what we'll share. I love you, I want you. This is *our* night. Please?"

John-Trevor's control snapped, and he was lost in a raging sea of passion. He shoved aside the voice of reason in his head and kissed Paisley with searing intensity.

There was nothing beyond the heated haze that surrounded them in a web of passion. There was nothing but want and need and the knowledge that they loved. There was nothing but each other, and the lovemaking that was to come.

John-Trevor broke the kiss to lift Paisley into his arms. He strode across the room and into the bedroom, which glowed faintly from the light spilling in from the living room.

He set her on her feet, then swept back the blankets on the bed. Framing her face in his hands, he gazed directly into her eyes.

"Are you positive that you . . ."

"Yes," she murmured.

He kissed her gently, reverently, and Paisley shivered. Slowly, so slowly, he removed her clothes, kissing and caressing each area of her dewy skin as it came into his smoldering view. His heated gaze lingered for a moment on the pale blue satin teddy she wore, as though he were etching the seductive image of her in his mind for all time. Then, with visibly shaking hands, he skimmed the laced-edged garment from her body.

Her small breasts were perfectly formed, round and firm and tempting. He cupped them in his palms, then lowered his head to lave one nipple, then the other, with his tongue, bringing them to taut points.

He moved lower, paying homage to every inch of her, until Paisley was trembling, her knees threatening to give way. Then he lifted her onto the cool sheets and swiftly shed his clothes.

As he stretched out beside her, resting on one arm, Paisley visually traced his body from head to toe, an expression of awe, of wonder, of desire and love, showing clearly on her face and radiating from her eyes.

She lifted one hand toward him, then hesitated, looking at him questioningly.

"I'm yours," he said, not recognizing the sound of his raspy voice. "All yours, Paisley."

She smiled, then tentatively drew her fingertips through the moist auburn curls on his chest. His soft groan encouraged her, and bolder, she explored him, marveling at the tautness of his warm skin, the rock-hard muscles beneath. He was fully aroused, yet she felt no trepidation at the thought of his manhood entering her, filling her, making them one.

She crowded her senses with the varying textures of John-Trevor's magnificent body, inhaled his aroma of soap, after-shave, and man, flicked her tongue across one shoulder and savored the salty taste of his skin.

Beads of sweat dotted John-Trevor's brow, and a moan rumbled in his chest as he mustered his control, willing himself not to move, determined that he wouldn't rush Paisley.

The expression on her face was one he would never forget—an intriguing combination of nearly childlike awe and desire so womanly, so raw and heated, that her gaze at times seemed to sear his skin.

He had never in his life felt so totally male, so acutely aware of his own virility and strength. Yet he also felt vulnerable, exposed.

Not by his nakedness, but by the realization that despite his physical power, he was capable of being crushed by the delicate woman he was gazing at.

But that was love.

And it was no longer quite so frightening, because it had stepped from the shadows and revealed itself to him. Its name was Paisley Kane.

He skimmed a shaking hand along her leg, then across her flat stomach to splay his fingers there, imagining their child growing safely within someday. As Paisley's busy hands continued to discover the mysteries of all that he was, he inched his own hand lower, then lower, finding her moist heat that gave evidence of her desire for him.

He kissed her deeply, then met her gaze, his eyes never leaving hers as he moved over her.

"I love you," he said hoarsely.

"Yes. Yes, and I love you."

He entered her slowly, holding himself in check, watching her face for any hint of pain. She wrapped her arms around his back and looked into his eyes. He saw trust there, along with desire. He pressed on.

"Hold tight," he said.

He gritted his teeth and thrust into her, forcing past nature's barrier, feeling her tense, hearing her gasp. He stopped, his muscles quivering. After an endless moment, Paisley relaxed and sighed; a soft sigh, a womanly sigh, that was matched by a lovely smile.

He slowly pulled back and thrust again, watching as her eyes widened, then began darkening with growing passion. Quickening his pace, he moved deeper within her, giving her all that he was as a man. She received him with all that she was as a woman, glorying in the beauty of what they were sharing, marveling at the perfect synchronization of their rocking bodies.

Deeper and deeper. Harder and faster. Heat. Coiling heat that seemed to lift them away from the here and now and fling them far beyond reality into a paradise of ecstasy.

"Oh! John-Trevor!"

As Paisley's body tightened around him in rippling spasms, John-Trevor joined her in the place that was theirs alone. He threw back his head and groaned in pure male pleasure, closing his eyes to savor the shudders of release sweeping through him. His life's force was drawn from him, and along with it, his strength. He collapsed against her.

She held him tightly as she floated in Paradise, then slowly, reluctantly, returned to reality. John-Trevor carefully shifted off her, tucked her close to his side, then pulled up the blankets.

"Paisley, I . . ." he started, then stopped.

His throat tightened and his eyes burned, and he knew that if he attempted to put into words how emotionally moved he was by their lovemaking, tears would fill his eyes and he'd be unable to keep them from flowing down his face.

Paisley placed the fingertips of one hand on his cheek with a featherlike touch and smiled. She was innocence lost and womanhood found, and she was so very much in love.

She knew as she gazed at John-Trevor that he was as deeply moved by their lovemaking as she was. Her eyes misted with tears. She made no attempt to blink them away, or to dash them from her cheeks where they sparkled like tiny diamonds in the dim glow from the lamps in the living room.

"I love you," John-Trevor said.

"And I love you," she answered.

No further words were spoken, but none were needed.

Paisley closed her eyes, floating on a cloud of sated contentment and happiness. Sleep claimed her as she lay in the warm, safe haven of John-Trevor's arms.

He watched her sleep. He lay perfectly still so as not to disturb her and simply gazed at her, filling his senses with the very essence of her. Time passed unnoticed as he held his Paisley.

But reality and reason were not to be ignored any longer, and nagging voices gathered force in his head, refusing to be dismissed again.

He'd have to take Paisley home soon, he knew, or the nutty group living in her house would probably call out the Marines. And he had to face the glaring fact that there *was* a world waiting out there, a world that contained Colonel William Blackstone. Paisley did not yet comprehend what the emergence of her father into her life meant. She didn't understand the magnitude of the changes that would take place if she stepped forth as the colonel's daughter.

Without realizing he had done it, John-Trevor tightened his hold on Paisley, causing her to stir before settling back to sleep. He buried his face in the dark halo of her hair and felt a cold knot of fear tighten in his gut.

Even as much as they loved each other, there was a frightening chance that he might lose her to a world that was beyond his reach.

For the first time in his life, he was in love, with nothing left to protect him from having his dreams for the future shattered. He had not had the wisdom to rest gently on those dreams. Delicate Paisley, so small, so fragile, held him in her power.

Yes, she loved him, but she had choices to make, decisions that could have tremendous effects on his life.

He could lose his Paisley, and the mere thought of it caused him to be consumed by a dark, heavy cloak of loneliness.

Nine

The next night, John-Trevor drove through the after-work rush-hour traffic toward Paisley's house. He hadn't seen her all day, not since he'd taken her home sometime around two A.M., after making slow, sweet love to her again.

He'd kissed her at her front door, she'd mumbled sleepily that she loved him, and he'd smiled as he saw her touch the stained-glass panel before she entered the house.

He was certain their love now held a place in the stained-glass panel, in the rainbow of dreams. He liked knowing that, although it was rather disconcerting to discover that hidden within him had been a romantic, sentimental man just waiting to surface.

He frowned as he parked in front of Paisley's house. There were still, he knew, several obstacles to overcome before his future life with Paisley was a given.

And the biggest problem was Colonel Blackstone. No, that wasn't fair, John-Trevor decided as he got out of the car. The colonel shouldn't be labeled a "problem." After all, the man had just discovered he had a lovely daughter and was hoping to be granted the opportunity to take his place in her life, claim the role he'd been denied for twenty-four years.

It was Paisley herself who had the ability to untangle the complicated web that had caught so many people. All he could do was stand by and wait.

He walked slowly toward the front porch, recalling the quick telephone call he'd received that morning from her. She'd like to go see Colonel Blackstone, please, she'd said. He'd agreed to make the arrangements and would pick her up after work. She'd said that she loved him, and that had been that.

It had been a long day.

Before he reached the steps, Paisley opened the front door. She was wearing tan corduroy slacks and her puffy red jacket. John-Trevor's heart did the two-step, and he opened his arms to her.

"Come here," he said.

She laughed, ran down the steps, and flung herself into his arms.

"I'm here," she said, smiling up at him.

"It's about time. Lord, I missed you today."

Any reply that Paisley might have made was silenced by a long, searing kiss that left them both breathless.

When he released her, Paisley drew much-needed air into her lungs, then said, "I met you outside because Maxine and the puppies came home today and Bobby is being very protective of them. It's so cute, but I wasn't sure you'd appreciate having to put on a surgical mask the moment you stepped inside. Gracie dyed her hair to celebrate Maxine's coming home. It's a strange shade of green, *really* strange, but Bobby told her it was awesome. The professor is muttering about inventing doggy dishes made out of biscuits so that when the puppies get bigger, they can eat their dinner and then gobble up the dish, resulting in less work for Bobby. It's an interesting thought, but . . . Oh, dear, John-Trevor, I'm so nervous about going to see Colonel Blackstone."

John-Trevor did a quick mental run-through of everything Paisley had said, realized to his amazement and delight that he'd comprehended all of it, then brushed his lips over hers.

"It's understandable that you're nervous," he said. Hell, so was he. "I imagine he's a bit uptight about this visit too. Let's get going. It's cold out here."

When they were both settled in the car, John-Trevor reached to turn the key in the ignition, then stopped.

"Nope," he said.

"Nope?" she echoed, looking over at him.

He turned, slid one hand to the nape of her neck, and leaned forward to capture her lips with his.

Hello again, John-Trevor, Paisley's heart sang. Oh, he tasted so good, looked magnificent, and she'd missed him so very much throughout the seemingly endless day.

He slowly raised his head. "Thanks. I needed that." He paused, a frown knitting his auburn brows. "Paisley, I have to know this, okay? You were so foggy with sleep last night when I brought you home, and you had to keep your telephone call to me today short, and I haven't had a chance to ask you if . . . well, if you're all right about last night, about the fact that we . . . that is, if you want to talk about it or . . ."

She smiled. "John-Trevor, your concern is very touching. But I have no regrets about our making love. None. It was wonderful, beyond my fantasies of what it would be like. I love you, John-Trevor, with all my heart. What we shared was glorious." She winked saucily. "Let's do it again."

He chuckled, then straightened and started the car. "Count on it." He met her gaze for a long moment, his smile fading. "I love you so very much."

"I'm glad you do. 'Glad' is too weak a word, but I hope you know what I mean."

He nodded, then pulled away from the curb.

Neither of them spoke as they turned their thoughts inward. They soon left the tangle of traffic behind and drove away from the city, into the mountains. Eventually, John-Trevor turned off the highway onto a road that wound upward. Soon the twinkling lights of Denver disappeared, leaving them in total darkness.

They traveled on a flat stretch for several miles, then John-Trevor stopped.

"Look," he said, pointing at the windshield. "That's Colonel Blackstone's house up there."

Paisley sat forward. "My goodness, it's enormous. I can't see it very clearly in the dark, but there are so many lights and . . ."

"He designed it himself," John-Trevor said. "That's just one of his many talents. It's set into the side of the mountain as though the house were there first, and the mountain rushed in to surround it. It's built in three staggered levels, each having a redwood deck. The windows in every room stretch from floor to ceiling with a spectacular view in all directions. It's huge but homey, comfortable and welcoming. George has his own set of rooms, and a housekeeper who also cooks comes in each day. The colonel has been asked by several architecture and interior design magazines to allow them to do articles with pictures about the place, but he always refuses. That house is his haven."

John-Trevor put the car into motion again, and Paisléy's gaze remained riveted on the lights of the distant house.

Oh, *mon Dieu,* she thought. She wanted to tell John-Trevor to turn around and take her back to the city, to her house, to her *world.* She wanted to grab him and run, allowing nothing, nor anyone, to intrude on their love, their future happiness together.

But she couldn't do so, because Col. William Blackstone was her father. *Her father.* He was the man who had caused the soft glow in her mother's eyes when she spoke of him, made her mother smile in a secret, special way as she relived cherished memories. He had given her the stained-glass panel, her rainbow of dreams. Colonel Blackstone was the man her mother had loved, and Paisley was the result of that love.

And now she had to decide what place the colonel would have in *her* life. Father. It sounded foreign, because fathers had always been what others had. Yet here he was, her father. And here also was John-Trevor, her love, her life. Oh, dear Lord, it was so much to handle all at once.

John-Trevor wove his way up the mountain, the lights of the house glowing brighter, finally revealing its actual tremendous size. He followed a circular drive around to the front and stopped.

"Ready?" he asked.

She hesitated only for a moment. "Yes."

He reached across the seat and gripped her hand.

"You're not alone, Paisley," he said, his voice low and gentle. "We're a team now, two halves of a whole. I'm right here for whatever you need. If you'd like to speak with the colonel privately, that's fine."

"No. No, John-Trevor, I want you there, with me."

"Then that's where I'll be."

Hand in hand, they walked up the front steps and across the wide porch. John-Trevor rang the bell, and almost instantly George opened the door.

"Good evening, Miss Kane, Mr. Payton," he said. "Come in." They stepped into the wide, uncluttered entryway, the floor covered in parquet. "How are Maxine and the puppies?"

"Oh, they're doing fine," Paisley said, smiling. "The puppies are adorable, and Bobby is hovering over the little family."

"That's good," George said, nodding. "How is . . . Well, I mean, I was just wondering how Gracie is? She's a fine woman, that Gracie, and I thought I'd ask how she was and . . ." He cleared his throat.

"Gracie is her usual, bouncy self," Paisley said. Her hair is sort of green at the moment. Not any shade of green I've seen before, but definitely green. She dyed it to celebrate the homecoming of Maxine and the babies."

"Now, isn't that something?" George said, grinning. "Whatever shade of green her hair is, I bet it looks mighty good. Yes, sir, I bet it does. I . . . um . . . Well, you could pass on my best regards to Gracie if you happen to think of it."

"I certainly will do that, George," Paisley said.

George suddenly seemed to find the tips of his shoes extremely fascinating. "The colonel is in his favorite spot, Mr. Payton," he said, still concentrating on his shoes. "You go right on in." He turned and hurried away.

"Gracie and George?" John-Trevor murmured. "Now *that* would be an interesting couple." He shrugged. "Well, George Burns and *his* Gracie were a great team, so . . ." He glanced at Paisley. Her eyes were wide and staring, her skin pale, and he realized she hadn't heard a word he'd said. "Paisley, take a deep breath and relax. Everything is going to work out just fine, you'll see."

Fate, are you there? Paisley mentally called. No, she didn't think so. Fate had brought her as far as it could, and now the final decisions rested in her hands and weighed heavily on her soul.

John-Trevor placed one hand at the small of her back and gently urged her along the hall. They stopped at the doorway to a large room, and a gasp of pleasure whispered from Paisley's lips.

Without even having seen any of the other

rooms in the house, she instantly knew why this was the colonel's favorite. Enormous bookcases flanked each side of a flagstone fireplace, where a welcoming, crackling fire blazed. High-backed leather chairs faced the hearth, and other groupings of sofas and chairs dotted the plush chocolate-brown carpet. It was a wonderful room, perfect to curl up in on a cold winter day, or when summer sunshine filled it.

"Good evening, Colonel," John-Trevor said.

Colonel Blackstone instantly rose from his leather chair. He was wearing dark slacks and a maroon velvet smoking jacket with black satin lapels.

"Come in, come in," he said, smiling. "Paisley, please sit here next to me. John-Trevor, pull up another chair. May I get you something to drink?"

"No, thank you," Paisley and John-Trevor said at once.

Paisley sat down where instructed, feeling as though she had settled into a deliciously soft marshmallow. John-Trevor carried over a smaller easy chair and placed it next to her.

"Colonel," he said as both men sat down, "Paisley has asked me to stay here while the two of you talk. Is that acceptable to you?"

"Of course, John-Trevor." The colonel sighed. "This has been an admittedly long, anxious day, Paisley. I was convinced at times that the clocks, my watch, all had broken."

"Yes," she said quietly, "I felt that way too."

Ditto, John-Trevor thought. Lord, the tension in the room was nearly palpable. So many lives would be affected by what was said that evening. *His* life, *his* future, was involved, yet he could only observe, listen, give support to Paisley, loyalty to Colonel Blackstone, and keep his own big mouth shut. He had no control, and he didn't like it, not one damn bit.

"May I speak first?" Paisley said, her voice higher than usual. "I realize this is your home, and I don't mean to be rude, but . . ."

"Go right ahead, my dear," Colonel Blackstone said.

She took a deep breath. "I hope you can understand how difficult it's been for me to comprehend that I am, after all these years, meeting my father, a man I never expected to know. I have to keep repeating it in my mind like a litany . . . Colonel Blackstone is my father, Colonel Blackstone is my father. I look at you, I look in the mirror, but I see only me, and a resemblance to my mother. I'm not doubting for a moment that you *are* my father, it's just been hard to grasp."

"I understand," the colonel said. "I felt that way a few weeks ago when I first learned that I had a daughter."

"My mother," Paisley went on, "loved you very much. I'm sure you know that, but I wanted to say it to you myself. I truly believe that if she had ever chosen to marry, it would have been to you. She couldn't do it, though, because she was . . . she was like a wind, dancing from here to there, touching down to rest, then swirling off again. Yet, she was a wonderful mother, always there when I needed her, never too busy to listen or pay attention to me."

Colonel Blackstone nodded. "Kandi was a remarkable woman. I've never loved any woman but her. I hurt her, Paisley, I can't deny that. I was arrogant, assuming my wealth would gain me what I wanted. I was wrong. When I finally realized that Kandi was not mine to have, I left her out of love before I caused her any more pain. I'm truly grateful that she eventually came to cherish the good times we shared, instead of concentrating on my foolish actions at the end."

"I understand what you're saying. I've thought about all of this so much, and I keep repeating things in my mind in a never ending circle. Questions, questions, but no answers."

"What are your questions?"

"You are my father. I am your daughter. Why is that so complicated? Why the references to a new life-style, a new world you'll be giving me? If I don't accept your money, which I really don't need or want any more than my mother did, then we can simply proceed with getting to know each other."

"Oh, that it would be that easy," the colonel said with a sigh. "Paisley, as ridiculous as it is, the press thinks I'm newsworthy, particularly here in Colorado, where they seem to think I'm some sort of state mascot. Poor boy makes good, that sort of thing. Someone recognized me when I played waiter last night, and reporters have been phoning me constantly since then. I hate to tell you how many times I've had my number changed over the years, but they have a way of finding out the new one."

"What did you tell the reporters?" John-Trevor asked.

"George blithered on about that restaurant's and that particular table's having sentimental value to me due to a past romance. I'll come across as an eccentric, rich nutcase, but that's better than having them turn their attention to who was sitting at the table while I was conducting my charade."

"Not bad," John-Trevor said.

"The point is, Paisley," Colonel Blackstone continued, "if you're seen coming here often, or if I'm observed going to your house, the reporters will sniff around. They'll either decide I've taken a young lover, or they'll discover the truth. Even if you publicly state that you refuse to accept any of my money now, or even upon my death, no one would believe you. You'd be caught up in the circus that is so often the bane of wealthy people who are in the public eye."

"What you're saying is sounding very black-and-white," John-Trevor interjected.

"Either Paisley walks out of your life and doesn't come back, or goes for the whole nine yards. Because you are a very prominent man, there's just no middle ground here."

"Correct," the colonel said.

"I see," Paisley murmured, then turned her head to gaze at the fire.

Several minutes passed and no one spoke. John-Trevor and Colonel Blackstone stared at Paisley, who continued to stare at the fire.

"Colonel," she finally said, turning to meet his gaze, "do you remember a black satin dress that my mother had? It was strapless, the bodice very tight fitting, but the skirt was full, layers of filmy chiffon over a stiff underskirt. When she twirled the chiffon would swirl around, and it looked as though she were flying."

"Yes, I remember that dress. I was, in fact, the one who hired the designer, to design it especially for her."

Paisley smiled. "Maybe that's why she always told me it was her favorite dress. Some nights, when I was a little girl, she'd put it on just for me, and we'd dance around the room with Maman singing."

Colonel Blackstone nodded. "I can imagine that so clearly in my mind. I remember a time when I bought her a huge bouquet of flowers from a street vendor, and as we walked along, she gave everyone she saw a flower. Many smiles were born that day because of Kandi. Another time she . . ."

Paisley and the colonel continued to talk, sharing memories of Kandi Kane. John-Trevor stood and crossed the room to pour himself a brandy. He stood in the shadows, watching and listening, as daughter and father spoke of a woman who had meant so much to both of them, but whom John-Trevor had never known.

Instead of sipping the expensive liquor, he took a deep swallow, hoping the burning liquid would dispel the chill growing within him.

The bond between Paisley and Colonel Blackstone was nearly visible to him, silken threads pulling them closer and closer together. And he was being left to stand alone in the darkness.

If he hadn't fallen in love with Paisley, he'd have been delighted with the scene he was observing, would have patted himself on the back for a job well done. But he *had* come to love Paisley Kane, and it was beginning to seem like an ominous dark cloud hovering over him, instead of a burst of glorious sunshine.

Nearly an hour later, Colonel Blackstone stiffened in surprise. "My goodness, Paisley, we've been going on and on. Look at the time."

"It's been so wonderful," she said, "to share stories and memories of my mother with someone who loved her. I can't begin to tell you how much this evening has meant to me."

"And to me," the colonel said, smiling warmly. "I'm not going to dwell on the years lost to us, Paisley, because there's no point in it. I can only hope that you will be a part of my future, my remaining days. Have you . . . have you reached a decision as to what you wish to do about acknowledging me as your father?"

Every muscle in John-Trevor's body tightened, and his jaw ached from clenching it. He set the brandy snifter on the table, his gaze fixed on Paisley.

"It's no longer a question waiting for an answer," she said. "You *are* my father, and I *am* your daughter. Whatever may flow from everyone's knowing about us will be dealt with as it comes. I can't walk out of your life now that we've found each other. That would be as impossible as my walking out of John-Trevor's life." She looked at the chair where he'd been sitting, only then realizing he had moved. "John-Trevor?"

"I'm here." He walked slowly forward to stand beside the fire, leaning one forearm on the mantel.

Colonel Blackstone gripped Paisley's hands, smiling hugely. "I will never forget this night!" he exclaimed. "I have a daughter. A daughter! And it would appear," he added, glancing at John-Trevor, "I'm to have a son-in-law as well."

"That's the plan," John-Trevor said somberly. "I haven't officially asked Paisley to marry me, but we're very much in love."

"This calls for champagne," the colonel said, getting to his feet.

Paisley also stood. "William, please, wait a minute. Gracie, Bobby, and the professor are part of my family too. Oh, and Maxine."

"*Our* family, Paisley," he said. "Don't worry about anyone or anything tonight. We'll take care of details later. Right now, a celebration is in order. I'll have George join us and we'll drink a toast to a bright and happy future." Still smiling, he left the room.

Paisley went to John-Trevor, wrapped her arms around his waist, and leaned her head on his chest. He embraced her.

"John-Trevor," she said, "I feel as though I'm having a wondrous dream, and I never want to wake up. Are we really going to be married?"

"Yes," he said quietly. "Well, if you accept my proposal."

She hugged him. "Of course I do. I love you. Everything is happening so quickly, but I refuse to worry about anything now. This night is too special. I love you so much. And the frosting on my beautiful cake is that I have a father who is glad that I'm his daughter. My rainbow of dreams is brilliant. I'm so happy, John-Trevor, so very, very happy."

He dropped a quick kiss on the top of her head. "Good. You deserve to be happy. That's the way it should be." He tightened his hold on her, and she sighed in contentment as she snuggled closer to him.

But John-Trevor stared across the room at nothing, the knot of fear in his gut growing bigger and more painful with every beat of his thundering heart.

Being in love, he thought dismally, was exactly as he'd always imagined it to be. Terrifying.

Ten

"Miss Kane," the first reporter on the library steps asked, "is it true that you and John-Trevor Payton ran off to Las Vegas to have a quickie wedding?"

"Where do you plan to live, Miss Kane?" another asked, pushing forward. "With Colonel Blackstone's money at your disposal, you have your choice of anywhere in the world."

"Will the colonel be living with you and Mr. Payton? Did you marry? If not, when is the wedding going to be?"

"What about the people presently living in your house? Will they continue to stay with you as . . . charity cases?"

"Is it true that Mr. Payton has returned to Los Angeles? Did you two have a lovers' quarrel?"

"Please, no more," Paisley said, blinking

away sudden tears. "You're all blocking the doors to the library and people can't get in. The directors of the library have asked me to take a leave of absence because you reporters have hounded me continually during the past three weeks since the colonel's press conference, and you've totally disrupted the tranquillity of the library. Can't you leave me alone? Please?"

"You're America's Sweetheart, Miss Kane," the reporter closest to her said. "The public is interested in everything you do. Is your hair naturally curly?"

"I must go," Paisley said, trying to circumvent the throng. "Please, let me through."

"One more question, Miss Kane . . ."

She stopped, her eyes flashing with anger as she looked at each reporter, one by one.

"No," she said. "*No* more questions. None. You're turning this into a nightmare, invading private lives to the point that we don't have a moment's peace. I'm going to my car, and I'm asking—no, I'm *demanding* that you don't take one more step toward me. Is that clear? Good day." She spun around and stomped off, her nose tilted in the air.

The reporters stayed where they were, watching her stalk across the parking lot.

"Whew," one man said. "She's got a temper when she puts it in gear."

"No joke," another man said. "I'm backing off for today, but this is too hot a story to let go. She'll cool off, get used to being in the limelight. The public is going nuts for this Cinderella bit. My editor would have my butt if I dropped the ball."

"Damn right. She'd better resign herself to being big news. Come on, guys, let's go have a beer."

Stopped at a red light, Paisley dashed fresh tears from her cheeks. *Qu'ai je fait?* she thought. What had she done? Her life was frighteningly out of control. Colonel Blackstone's idea to have a press conference to announce that he'd discovered, to his infinite joy, that he had a daughter, thus giving the reporters the true story once in its entirety, had backfired. What the colonel had hoped to be a front-page newsflash, then forgotten by the next day, had mushroomed into a hideous, ever-growing wave of excitement.

It was like a bad movie, she thought dismally as the light turned green and she drove on. There seemed to be reporters everywhere, yelling at her, pushing microphones in her face, taking her picture. Then today she'd been called into her supervisor's office and told that it would be best for all concerned if she took a leave of absence until things calmed down.

"Oh, damn, damn," she muttered.

And she missed John-Trevor so much. When he'd left ten days ago, he'd said he didn't want to go, but serious matters awaited his attention at his office in Los Angeles. They'd hardly had any time alone in the week and a half before he'd left, though they had managed to sneak through the kitchen of his hotel on several occasions to get to his room.

A soft smile touched Paisley's lips. There, with the door closed against the world, they had made exquisite love and had felt as though they were the only two people in the universe. But all too soon, they had to emerge to face once more the badgering reporters.

As the days passed, John-Trevor had had difficulty keeping his temper in check. He'd come very close to punching a particularly pushy reporter. Even before he'd flown back to California, he'd seemed to be withdrawing from her, becoming more tense and quiet each day. She could hardly remember the last time he'd smiled or laughed right out loud.

Paisley parked in front of the house and looked quickly around, relieved that no reporters were in sight. She hurried up the walk, pulled open the storm door, then stopped, her troubled gaze on the stained-glass panel.

She lifted one trembling hand to touch the sparkling glass, then hesitated, a sob catching in her throat.

"Oh, my God, John-Trevor," she whispered, tears spilling over. It was falling apart, everything, being destroyed by strangers who were trying to dissect them, as if they were butterflies trapped under a microscope. There had to be a way to stop this madness before it was too late.

She placed her fingertips gently on the glass.

"John-Trevor," she whispered, "I love you so very, very much. But now that I've taken care of everyone else, what am I going to do about myself?"

The three Payton brothers were about the same height and build, and each had sky-blue eyes framed by thick lashes. The major difference between them was the color of their hair. While John-Trevor's was dark auburn, Paul-Anthony, the eldest, had hair as black as coal, with threads of silver at the temples. James-Steven, the youngest, had sun-streaked blond hair, usually in need of a trim.

Paul-Anthony frowned as he stared at John-Trevor, who was slouched in a chair opposite the desk, talking about all that had happened since he'd left for Denver a month before.

"It's an incredible story," Paul-Anthony said when his brother finally finished. "I've been reading about you in the papers, but figured it was mostly hype. If you didn't look as though you hadn't slept in the ten days you've been back in L.A., I'd be inclined to think you're pulling my leg. Why didn't you come to me sooner and get this off your chest?"

"I needed some time alone," John-Trevor said. "Besides, you and Alida are still on cloud nine about Chris-Noel's being born on Christmas Day. I didn't want to dump my troubles on you now."

"Dammit, John-Trevor, that's what brothers are for. I realize that James-Steven and Maggie are still on vacation in Ireland, visiting her family, but I'm here, and I didn't even know you were back in town. What I also can't understand is why you haven't called Paisley since you left Denver."

John-Trevor pushed himself out of the chair and strode to the huge windows that gave a sweeping view of Los Angeles. A heavy smog hung over the city in a smoky, yellow blanket.

"I've wanted to talk to Paisley," he said quietly. "I miss her so damn much, but . . ." He turned and faced his brother. "It's been a circus ever since the colonel's press conference. I've been with Paisley and the colonel. I've seen the smile on her face when they share memories of her mother."

"So?"

"We've had dinner at the colonel's house, and I've heard Paisley rave about the beautiful crystal, the china that's so fine and thin you can practically see through it. One night

Colonel Blackstone started reminiscing about places he'd traveled to, especially Paris, and Paisley hung on every word, forgetting I was even in the room. The colonel is giving her glimpses of his world, what he can offer her. How in the hell am I supposed to compete with that?"

"You and Paisley are in love," Paul-Anthony said. "The fact that you've fallen in love is amazing in itself. The thing is, you don't yet understand the power of love, how strong it is when two people join forces and become a united front. Give Paisley some credit here, John-Trevor. Have you bothered to ask her how she's feeling about all of this, what her reactions are to the realization that the world is at her fingertips because Colonel Blackstone is her father?"

"No, we haven't talked about it because . . . well, there hasn't been time, any chance to talk. The press is going nuts. The reporters hounded us day and night."

"Yes, I can tell that by the continuing front-page stories about this," Paul-Anthony said. "I sure as hell didn't know you've been hiding out here in L.A., though."

"I'm not hiding," John-Trevor nearly yelled. "I'm getting out of Paisley's way so she can attempt to view this mess objectively. I can't begin to give her what Colonel Blackstone can, and I won't stand in her way if she . . . Ah, hell, don't you see? I never intended to fall in love, strip myself emotionally bare, and here I am in love with Paisley. Okay, she loves me, but that's no guarantee we'll be able to have a future together. It's all so complicated and . . ."

"Frightening?" Paul-Anthony said quietly. "Is that what this is all about, John-Trevor? Have you gotten cold feet? Are you plain old scared to death because you've gone down a road you never intended to travel?"

"Paul-Anthony, shut up."

"Fine," Paul-Anthony said, raising both hands. "You'd better think about what I said, though. You're trying to dump all this on Paisley, and the colonel too. I'd suggest you look a little closer to home."

"You're so full of bull," he said, striding toward the door. He stopped and turned to look at his brother again. "The problem is that Paisley's being jerked back and forth between what I can give her and what Colonel Blackstone has to offer." He shook his head. "Forget it. I'm going back to Denver."

"Wait. What are you going to do?"

"I'll—I'll tell you later, Paul-Anthony. I've got to get going." He laughed, a humorless, hollow sound. "History repeats itself. That's not an old wives' tale, it's actually true. History does repeat itself. I'll see you."

"Dammit, what—" Paul-Anthony threw up his hands as his brother slammed the door closed. "Damn."

* * *

Late that afternoon, John-Trevor stepped up onto the porch of Paisley's house. The day was unusually warm. There was no snow, and birds chirped as if calling to the fluffy clouds dotting the blue sky. It was a lovely day in Denver, but John-Trevor Payton didn't give a damn.

He pulled open the storm door, then stiffened so quickly, his muscles ached from the sudden tension. A roaring noise echoed in his ears, and his heart beat painfully hard.

The stained-glass panel was gone.

"Oh, God," he whispered, staring at the ugly cardboard that had taken its place.

His hand trembling, he pressed the doorbell. "Here Comes Peter Cottontail" rang out, then the door was opened.

Paisley.

In black slacks and a bright red sweater, the stained-glass panel clutched to her breasts, she stood staring at him with her big, dark eyes.

I love you! he shouted silently. "May I come in?" he asked.

She stepped back and he entered. Padded paper littered the hallway floor, no doubt to wrap the stained glass in. He met Paisley's gaze again.

"You're obviously leaving," he said, his voice thick and strained. "You're moving to the colonel's, right? Into his home, his life, his world."

"John-Trevor, I—"

He raised one hand to silence her. "Look, I understand, I really do. I told my brother Paul-Anthony that history repeats itself, and that's what's happening here."

"But—"

"Let me finish, all right? Twenty-five years ago, Colonel Blackstone walked out of Kandi Kane's life because he loved her so much, he placed her happiness before his own. She wanted a life far different from what he was offering her, and he respected that. He loved her enough to leave her."

John-Trevor swallowed heavily past the lump in his throat.

"And now," he went on, "history repeats itself. I love you, Paisley. I love you so damn much that I'm going to walk out of your life. You've obviously decided to go to your father, and it's okay. It's okay, Paisley, because you deserve what he can give you. I came here because I wanted to say it in person. Don't feel guilty, promise me you won't. I'll be fine, really. Being in love is a heavy trip, and I'm not all that sure I can handle it. So, I want you to be happy, the way you should be."

Paisley set the stained-glass panel on the small table beside the door, leaning it against the glass that still framed the door, then looked back up at John-Trevor.

"I'd better go," he said. "Have a wonderful life and . . . Good-bye, Paisley." He reached for the doorknob.

"John-Trevor Payton," she said, "if you

walk out that door, I'll slam-dunk you into a snowdrift as soon as there's a snowdrift to slam-dunk you into. Don't you move, until I've had my say."

He blinked, opened his mouth, shut it, then dropped his hand from the doorknob and turned to face her.

"First of all, Mr. Payton," she said, determinedly lifting her chin and wishing to the heavens that her voice wasn't so unsteady, "you are a rotten bum for not contacting me for the past ten days."

"I—"

"Quiet."

"Oh."

"That was really lousy of you, and I don't appreciate it one little bit. There, we've covered that. After you left I felt so defeated by everything and was a total wreck because the reporters wouldn't leave me alone. I was caught up in a nightmare that seemed to have no end. So, I gave fate a holiday and took matters into my own hands."

John-Trevor's gaze slid to the stained-glass panel, then back to Paisley.

"That's evident," he said.

"Do not, sir, interrupt me again."

"Right."

"Where was I? Oh, yes, taking matters into my own hands. I met with my father a couple of days ago, and we had a long, lovely talk. I then held a meeting here with the whole family, including Maxine, of course, and I presented my idea to them. My father has an enormous house, as you well know, and—"

"Paisley, please," John-Trevor said. "This is rough enough without hearing every detail of how you reached the decision to go live with your father. You knew, you had to, that I'm my own man, that I wouldn't accept any of the colonel's money when you and I married. You've made your choice. Let's not beat this to death. It's over."

She planted her fists on her hips and narrowed her eyes. "The hell it is, Payton."

He gaped at her in surprise.

"Oh, John-Trevor," she said, her tone gentling, "I'm not only listening to you, but I'm hearing, really hearing, what you're saying. You never intended to fall in love, but you did, and it became a tangled web so quickly, because of my meeting my father. You're protecting yourself against what you now believe is guaranteed pain. My darling, I had moments of fear too."

"You? But you *wanted* to fall in love, Paisley."

"Yes, I did. I hoped that fate would grant me that dream. But during these past few weeks there were times when it was so overwhelming, and I was so afraid there wasn't enough of me to go around, that I couldn't have it all. It must have been horrible for you, because you didn't want to fall in love in the first place. I'm so sorry, John-Trevor, that I didn't look beyond my own turmoil to see how very difficult this has all been for you. No wonder you're ready to walk away from me. No wonder you got cold feet and decided to call it quits."

"Hey," he said, frowning, "have you been talking to Paul-Anthony?"

"No, and would you just shut up and listen?"

"Oh."

"John-Trevor Payton, I love you. I love you first and foremost, forsaking all others, until death parts us. You are my rainbow of dreams, every color, except for the one I keep for our bushel of babies. I told my father that, and he understood, said it was how it should be. But then we talked on, and he admitted he was lonely, and I admitted that I was worried about leaving my little family with no one to watch over them, and we agreed, and they agreed, and . . . they moved to William's house yesterday, Gracie, the professor, Bobby, Maxine, and the puppies."

"But—"

"You should see them. They're all wonderfully happy. George is so smitten with Gracie. Gracie is in seventh heaven in that kitchen. Bobby is in charge of Colonel Blackstone's fleet of vintage cars, and they're planning to drive one together in a classic-car parade. The professor has a huge room to tinker in, and Maxine and the babies are being spoiled rotten. There's laughter and sunshine in that house, John-Trevor. You can hear and feel it the moment you walk in the front door."

"And—and you? What about you, Paisley?" he asked, hardly breathing.

"I didn't hear from you, John-Trevor, not for ten lonely, miserable days." Tears filled her eyes. "But I couldn't believe that fate had been wrong, I just refused to accept that you didn't love me, that you had left me forever. Oh, darling, don't you see? I took my stained-glass panel out of the door so I could bring it with me when I came to Los Angeles. I was coming to *you*. I wasn't moving to my father's house."

"Paisley?"

"The reporters will leave us alone after a while, once they realize I'm not living the life-style of Colonel Blackstone's daughter, but that of your wife, the mother of your children. Colonel Blackstone and his new family are much more interesting than we will be. We'll visit them on holidays, see my father for special events as any married daughter would. Do you understand now? Is it what you want? I'm yours, John-Trevor, from this day forward, if that is still what's in your heart." A sob caught in her throat. "I love you so much, so very, very much."

With a groan John-Trevor pulled her into his arms, holding her so tightly she could hardly breathe.

"I've been playing mind games, I guess," he said. "I'd convinced myself that I should leave you as the colonel left your mother. But now I see that I was simply scared. I was running from myself, not from you. Paisley, will you marry me? Will you be my wife, have a bushel of babies with me?"

"Yes. Oh, yes."

She tilted her head back to look up at him, and her heart nearly burst with love when she saw the tears shimmering in his blue eyes. She smiled at him, then he lowered his head and kissed her, sealing their commitment to a lifetime together. The world beyond the two of them was forgotten.

And then, as though fate demanded to have the final word, the sun burst from behind a wayward cloud and poured over the stained-glass panel.

Sparkling, vibrant colors cascaded over Paisley and John-Trevor like a waterfall, a beautiful rainbow of wonderful dreams.

THE EDITOR'S CORNER

Each month we have LOVESWEPTs that dazzle . . . that warm the heart or bring laughter and the occasional tear—all of them sensual and full of love, of course. Seldom, however, are all six books literally sizzling with so much fiery passion and tumultuous romance as next month's.

First, a love story sure to blaze in your memory is remarkable Billie Green's **STARBRIGHT,** LOVESWEPT #456. Imagine a powerful man with midnight-blue eyes and a former model who has as much heart and soul as she does beauty. He is brilliant lawyer Garrick Fane, a man with a secret. She is Elise Adler Bright, vulnerable and feisty, who believes Garrick has betrayed her. When a terrifying accident hurls them together, they have one last chance to explore their fierce physical love . . . and the desperate problems each has tried to hide. As time runs out for them, they must recapture the true love they'd once believed was theirs—or lose it forever. Fireworks sparked with humor. A sizzler, indeed.

Prepare to soar when you read LOVESWEPT #457, **PASSION'S FLIGHT,** by talented Terry Lawrence. Sensual, sensual, sensual is this story of a legendary dancer and notorious seducer known throughout the world as "Stash." He finds the woman he can love faithfully for a lifetime in Mariah Heath. Mariah is also a dancer and one Stash admires tremendously for her grace and fierce emotionality. But he is haunted by a past that closes him to enduring love—and Mariah must struggle to break through her own vulnerabilities to teach her incredible lover that forever can be theirs. This is a romance that's as unforgettable as it is delectable.

As steamy as the bayou, as exciting as Bourbon Street in New Orleans, **THE RESTLESS HEART**, LOVESWEPT #458, by gifted Tami Hoag, is sure to win your heart. Tami has really given us a gift in the hero she's created for this romance. What a wickedly handsome, mischievous, and sexy Cajun Remy Doucet is! And how he woos heroine Danielle Hamilton. From diapering babies to kissing a lady senseless, Remy is masterful. But a lie and a shadow stand between him and Danielle . . . and only when a dangerous misunderstanding parts them can they find truth and the love they deserve. Reading not to be missed!

Guaranteed to start a real conflagration in your imagination is extraordinary Sandra Chastain's **FIREBRAND**, LOVESWEPT #459. Cade McCall wasn't the kind of man to answer an ad as mysterious as Rusty Wilder's—but he'd never needed a job so badly. When he met the green-eyed rancher whose wild red hair echoed her spirit, he fell hard. Rusty found Cade too handsome, too irresistible to become the partner she needed. Consumed by the flames of desire they generated, only searing romance could follow . . . but each feared their love might turn to ashes if he or she couldn't tame the other. Silk and denim . . . fire and ice. A LOVESWEPT that couldn't have been better titled—**FIREBRAND**.

Delightful Janet Evanovich outdoes herself with **THE ROCKY ROAD TO ROMANCE**, LOVESWEPT #460, which sparkles with fiery fun. In the midst of a wild and woolly romantic chase between Steve Crow and Daisy Adams, you should be prepared to meet an old and fascinating friend—that quirky Elsie Hawkins. This is Elsie's fourth appearance in Janet's LOVESWEPTs. All of us have come to look forward to where she'll turn up next . . . and just how she'll affect the outcome of a stalled romance. Elsie won't disappoint you as she works her wondrous ways on the smoldering romance of Steve and Daisy. A real winner!

Absolutely breathtaking! A daring love story not to be missed! Those were just a couple of the remarks heard in the office from those who read **TABOO,** LOVESWEPT #461, by Olivia Rupprecht. Cammie Walker had been adopted by Grant Kennedy's family when her family died in a car crash. She grew up with great brotherly love for Grant. Then, one night when Cammie came home to visit, she saw Grant as she'd never seen him before. Her desire for him was overwhelming . . . unbearably so. And Grant soon confessed he'd been passionately in love with her for years. But Cammie was terrified of their love . . . and terrified of how it might affect her adopted parents. **TABOO** is one of the most emotionally touching and stunningly sensual romances of the year.

And do make sure you look for the three books next month in Bantam's fabulous imprint, FANFARE . . . the very best in women's popular fiction. It's a spectacular FANFARE month with **SCANDAL** by Amanda Quick, **STAR-CROSSED LOVERS** by Kay Hooper, and **HEAVEN SENT** by newcomer Pamela Morsi.

Enjoy!

Sincerely,

Carolyn Nichols

Carolyn Nichols,
Publisher,
LOVESWEPT
Bantam Books
666 Fifth Avenue
New York, NY 10103

THE LATEST IN BOOKS AND AUDIO CASSETTES

60 Minutes to a Better, More Beautiful You!

Now it's easier than ever to awaken your sensuality, stay slim forever—even make yourself irresistible. With Bantam's bestselling subliminal audio tapes, you're only 60 minutes away from a better, more beautiful you!

__ 45004-2	**Slim Forever**		$8.95
__ 45035-2	**Stop Smoking Forever**		$8.95
__ 45022-0	**Positively Change Your Life**		$8.95
__ 45041-7	**Stress Free Forever**		$8.95
__ 45106-5	**Get a Good Night's Sleep**		$7.95
__ 45094-8	**Improve Your Concentration**		$7.95
__ 45172-3	**Develop A Perfect Memory**		$8.95